Tattoos &

TATAS

Chocoholics #2.5

TARA SIVEC

Tattoos and TaTas
Copyright © 2014 Tara Sivec

Disclaimer

Editing by Nikki Rushbrook and Donna Soluri.

Cover Art by Lola Famure

Interior Design by Angela McLaurin, Fictional Formats
https://www.facebook.com/FictionalFormats

Also by Tara Sivec

Romantic Comedy
The Chocolate Lovers Series:
Seduction and Snacks (Chocolate Lovers #1)
Futures and Frosting (Chocolate Lovers #2)
Troubles and Treats (Chocolate Lovers #3)

The Chocoholics Series:
Love and Lists (Chocoholics #1)
Passion and Ponies (Chocoholics #2)
Tattoos and TaTas (Chocoholics #2.5) – Coming 10/1/2014

Romantic Suspense
The Playing With Fire Series:
A Beautiful Lie (Playing With Fire #1)
Because of You (Playing With Fire #2)
Worn Me Down (Playing With Fire #3)
Closer to the Edge (Playing With Fire #4)

Romantic Suspense/Erotica
The Ignite Trilogy
Burned (Ignite Trilogy Volume 1)
Branded (Ignite Trilogy Volume 2) – Coming Winter 2014
Scorched (Ignite Trilogy Volume 3) – Coming Spring 2015

New Adult Drama
Watch Over Me

Romantic Comedy/Mystery
The Fool Me Once Series:
Shame on You (Fool Me Once #1)
Shame on Me (Fool Me Once #2)
Shame on Him (Fool Me Once #3)
Closer to the Edge (Playing With Fire #4)

A Note to Readers

The idea for *Tattoos and TaTas* came to me about six months ago. It was a combination of things that made me want to write this story, first and foremost being that breast cancer awareness is something very near and dear to my heart. The second, it was the third anniversary of my mother's death from Leukemia. My family and I always reminisce about the time we spent together in hospital rooms, waiting rooms, emergency rooms and the ICU. Unlike most families, we're a bunch of assholes, so these memories are mostly happy, crazy, stupid ones.

I want everyone reading this to understand that I am in no way making light of breast cancer. It is a horrible disease that does not discriminate. It took my grandmother, one of my favorite cousins at a young age, infected several other family members and close friends and I myself had a scare a few years ago.

This story, as with the rest of the *Chocolate Lovers* and *Chocoholic* stories, is a way for me to share some real life events with all of you. It's my way of showing you that sometimes, it's okay to laugh, even when faced with something scary. Most of the events in this book are actual things my family and I did while my mom was sick. We're insane and we think we're funny when we're probably not, but it's our way of coping. I hope you enjoy *Tattoos and TaTas* and I hope it makes you laugh through the tears.

During the month of October, every single year, 100% of the proceeds from the sale of this book will be equally split between the Susan G. Komen Breast Cancer Foundation and Living Beyond Breast Cancer. During my research of this book, I found so many wonderful groups dedicated to breast cancer awareness that I decided to share the funds with more than one charity.

Research and statistics provided by the following sources:

www.breastcancer.org

www.komenohio.org

www.chemocare.com

www.lbbc.org

www.cancer.gov

www.cancerresearchuk.org

www.nationalbreastcancer.org

Tattoos &

TATAS

Chocoholics #2.5

In memory of those we've lost and in support of the survivors, the fighters and everyone who loves them.

"Through humor, you can soften some
of the worst blows that life delivers. And once you
find laughter, no matter how painful your situation
might be, you can survive it."
—Bill Cosby

Prologue

HAVE YOU EVER met someone who you instantly knew was meant to be in your life forever? I'm not talking about the guy you took home from the bar one night after eleventy-seven rum and Cokes. You know, the one who disappeared after making your vagina sing a lovely melody. I'm not even talking about the person you're dating, engaged to or that you married. Sure, some people find that one person they know they want to spend the rest of their life with, making babies and growing old together with, but I'm not talking about that. I'm talking about your soul mate. Your REAL soul mate. The person who was put on this earth just to *get* you, not to breed with you.

I met the love of my life, Jim, in college and I did all

those things that you're supposed to do with him. We fell in love, got married, had babies and lived happily ever after, but I found my soul mate much earlier than that. I met her in high school.

Oh, shut up, I'm not a lesbian. I'm talking about my best friend. My *person*. You might want to sit down for this next part because when I tell you how we met, I'm sure you'll fall over laughing your ass off. There will be no judging how Claire and I met or I will cut all of your mothers.

We met during cheerleading tryouts.

Shut up, I told you this is a judgment-free zone.

Commiserating over our fellow female students bouncing around and squealing exactly like cracked-out puppies brought us together, but our bond *kept* us together. We shared so many commonalities that it even freaked *us* out. Our parents shared the same wedding anniversary, somewhere in our ancient family tree we shared the same last name and family crest, my first name is her middle name and her first dog and I shared a name (I never met Liz the beagle, but I heard she was an asshole who licked her twat all the time. Sounds about right). We liked all the same movies and books and we finished each other's sentences. Claire and I met in the back of our high school gym, the only two girls in a group of thirty standing off on the sidelines with our arms crossed in front of us and similar resting-bitch faces plastered on.

We've been through everything together. Losing our virginities, college, starting a successful business, marriage, children, the imminent marriage *of* our children... through thick and thin and all the years in between, nothing could tear us apart.

Or so I thought.

Then that bitch had to go and give me the news that you never want to hear out of your best friend's mouth.

I can already hear all of you saying to yourself, "Awwwww shit, I wasn't expecting this; this is supposed to be funny and what you're about to put us through is NEVER funny." This is where I prove you wrong. The one thing this group has always had going for us is our sense of humor. Even when you get the worst news of your life, sometimes all you can do is laugh.

This is the story of the day everything changed, the day we all began looking at life a little differently than we did before.

It's also the story of how we almost got kicked out of a hospital, a funeral home, a tattoo shop and a small handful of bars.

So, basically just another Tuesday.

I feel like a little background is needed before we get into that whole crazy mess, though, so buckle up. It's going to be a bumpy ride.

Chapter 1

Go Ducks! Rrraaawwr!

Tenth day of eleventh grade.
Too many years ago to count...

I HATE MY mother. This is probably a little bit of PMS and a whole lot of teenage-angst talking right now, but whatever. I hate her and I will continue hating her until the day I die. Or until the day I smother her in her sleep, whichever comes first. Not only did my parents ruin my life by deciding halfway through my high school career that we should move to some podunk town in Ohio, they are now forcing me to participate in extracurricular activities or suffer the consequences.

Their consequences usually entail an entire month of being confined to the house I'm forced to clean from top to bottom every single day. Being in a new school and not having any friends yet, I wouldn't normally care about the whole grounding bit, but it's the principle of the thing. My parents are under the illusion that if I become a sheep and follow around all the other stupid sheep with the added bonus of wearing a matching uniform, I'll instantly have friends and will no longer spend my hours at home locked in my room playing "Teenage Wasteland" on repeat as well as watching my new favorite movie— *Heathers*. My mother seems to think my obsession with a dark comedy about teenagers killing each other off is not healthy. I beg to differ. I tried to reason with her that the movie is set in Ohio so really, I'm supporting this shitty state they've forced me to live in, but it didn't work. She confiscated my VHS and it's on lockdown until I find an after school activity.

My goal this week wasn't really about finding a group that would be fun, because any situation where I'm forced to interact with other people is never fun. My goal was simply to pick the first thing I saw to shut my mother up and pray to God I wouldn't die from boredom or start passing out cups of Liquid Drano to my fellow students (See? A *Heathers* reference. That movie really is sanity saving).

As I was grabbing a few books from my locker at the end of the day and in a total panic that I still hadn't found a flock of sheep to join, a group of girls walked by all in a tizzy about some meeting going on in the gym and how they were going to have such a fun year going to all the football games. My ears immediately perked up at this information. I'm a football junkie. I love watching it, I love playing it every Thanksgiving with my cousins and, if my mother didn't think wearing a football helmet would ruin my hair, I'd have demanded to play on the school team. This, ladies and gentlemen, is the only sport/activity that I truly would have joined the masses for without one complaint. Deciding to see what all the fuss was about, I trudged behind the group of girls and tried not to gag on the smell of Love's Baby Soft wafting from each of them.

By the time I entered the gym and my brain caught up with what I was seeing in front of me, it was already too late to turn and run. I'd been spotted; honed in on like a raw steak thrown into a cage of rabid dogs. The mortification written all over my face was like a lighthouse in a storm to the she-devil who immediately bombarded me.

"Oh, my God, I LOVE your hair! It's so pretty and blonde!"

I watched in horror as the perky brunette bounced up to me, her hand coming towards me like she wanted to pet my hair. I smacked it away with a frown, but that didn't deter her.

"You are so cute! My name's Candace, but everyone calls me Candy!" she told me excitedly.

"Candy? That's a stripper's name."

She stared at me blankly for a few seconds and then began giggling as she wrapped one hand around my elbow and started dragging me closer to the large group of girls bouncing up and down in the middle of the gym, clapping their hands and squealing so loudly that I'm pretty sure my ears were bleeding.

"You are going to be perfect for the top of the pyramid. You're so tiny and cute and everyone is going to love you! And since I'm the captain, I get to decide who makes the squad and who gets cut, so you're in luck!" Stripper Candy babbled.

Pyramid. Squad. Captain… Oh, fuck.

"Tell me this isn't cheerleading practice," I mumbled as half the girls noticed us walking towards them and turned their clapping and squealing in our direction.

"EEEEEEK someone new!"

"Candy, you are a genius. She HAS to be on the squad!"

"I get to braid her hair first!"

I'm pretty sure at this point my brain went into self-preservation mode like those people who are in horrible accidents and wake up with temporary amnesia. My mind refused to process what was happening, which is the only explanation for why I wasn't running out of here screaming like my head was on fire.

In case you haven't already realized this, I'm not a girly-girl. Most of my friends are guys because I just can't stand the drama that comes with having girlfriends. I don't doodle my name with some dude's last name all over my notebooks with hearts around them, I don't spend two hours getting ready to go out in public, I hate pop music and the last time I wore a dress was… actually, I've never worn a dress. I don't squeal, clap my hands or bounce up and down when I get excited, so obviously I'm in the wrong place right now. I am NOT cheerleader material.

"Touch my hair and die," I deadpan to a tall blonde with her hands dangerously close to my head.

"Isn't she just the best?!" Candy shrieks. "Who wants some bubble gum lip gloss?"

I cover my ears as the group starts screaming and reaching for the pink tube of gloss Candy pulled out of her cleavage. When the tube finally makes its way to me, I stare at it with a look of disgust on my face.

"I am not putting anything near my mouth that has *her* tit sweat on it," I inform them with a point in Candy's direction.

Someone blows a whistle and my faux pas of refusing Candy's tit gloss is forgotten as the girls race to the other side of the gym. In the wake of all that hyperactive estrogen, I see a girl standing directly across from me with her arms crossed in front of her, looking just as miserable as I am. Now, I'm not one of those girls who goes out of her way to make friends, which I think is pretty apparent by now. I've never taken it upon myself to make the first move—people always seem to come to me and I am perfectly okay with that. For the first time in the history of my seventeen years, I feel the need to approach someone and share my pain with this girl. No sooner have I decided to do something completely out of character for me, when she drops her arms and I get a good look at the t-shirt she's wearing. It's white, off the shoulder and, in giant red letters across the front, it reads "BIG FUN." It's almost like the heavens opened up above her and a light from the gods begins to shine down. Or it's just the fact that she moved under one of the gym lights, but whatever. I'm calling it a sign, thank you very much. It can't be a coincidence that this girl is wearing a Martha Dumptruck, *Heathers* shirt. Well, I guess it could. I mean, maybe she used to be a big girl and she lost a bunch of weight and she's trying to tell everyone that even though on the outside she's small, on the inside she's still big and full of fun.

Fuck it, I'm going in.

I make it across the gym to her right about the time that all the perky cheerleaders start shouting some stupid chant about the football team.

"Is this school's mascot really the Ducks?" I ask in shock as I stand next to her and we stare at the synchronized movements across the way.

"Yes, yes it is," she replies. "Last year, Candy decided that shouting 'quack' wasn't tough enough. She changed all of the cheers to "Let's go Ducks—RRRRWWWAAAAR!"

"Candy made ducks growl?"

She nods. "Candy made ducks growl. Candy is a dumb fuck."

"Don't take this the wrong way, but you don't really seem like the cheerleader type," I inform her.

She lets out a sigh and turns to face me. "Yeah, I could say the same for you. Nice effort on the stripper comment. Unfortunately, that really is what she wants to be when she grows up, so she definitely took it as a compliment."

She finally turns to face me, sticking her hand out in front of her. "I'm guessing you're new here? My name's Claire Morgan. Welcome to hell."

After listening to the Ducks growl for two minutes, we decided our time would be better spent hiding in the locker room until practice was over. I know this isn't exactly what my mother had in mind when she told me to be a joiner, but it was safer for all those annoying cheerleaders if we were as far away from them as possible. One more growl and Claire and I were going to start throwing punches.

We had an immediate connection and neither one of us was afraid to admit that it was weird. Like me, she mostly hated other people and kept to herself and her father forced her into joining the cheerleading squad because her mother moved away to "find herself" and he was afraid that, without some other female influence in her life, she would turn into a crazy cat lady or open fire at a post office one day.

I quickly found out her shirt was, in fact, a tribute to *Heathers* and we spent twenty minutes trading our favorite quotes. We agreed that "Fuck me gently with a chainsaw" was probably the best sentence ever uttered in the history of the world and, from that moment on, we never spent more than a few hours apart from each other.

My parents and her father weren't too thrilled with the fact that we quit the cheerleading squad before we'd even technically made the team, but Claire and I were geniuses when we banded together for a cause. They quickly realized that our friendship wasn't to be messed with and that as long as we weren't spending every waking moment of the rest of our high school lives alone in our rooms wallowing in misery, wearing all black and listening to The Cure, we would be okay. We had each other and nothing else mattered.

And that, boys and girls, is how the dynamic duo of Liz and Claire came to be. Next comes the part where you might want to put on that seatbelt I mentioned. Or grab a nice giant cup of vodka. You're going to need it.

Chapter 2

Who Wants Blistex?

Present Day

"SO, I HAVE cancer. Who wants more wine?" Claire states with a big smile.

I know it's probably not the most appropriate response to the words that just left my best friend's mouth, but I laugh.

And once I start, I can't stop. It could be due to the amount of wine Claire, Jenny and I have consumed tonight at our favorite bar, Fosters, or it could be the fact that, while this is the worst joke in the history of jokes, it still has to be a joke since Claire is smiling.

"Ooooh, I have something for that!" Jenny announces as she reaches for her purse on the empty seat next to her. After a few seconds of rummaging around, she holds out a tube of Blistex in Claire's direction.

"Why in the hell are you giving me Blistex?" Claire asks as she tops off her wine glass and empties our third bottle of the night.

Claire used to work at Fosters back when she was a single mother and the owners still adore her, so they let her go behind the bar whenever we're here and help herself to whatever she wants. Sometimes, it's a little dangerous that we never have to wait for a waitress to refill our glasses and I'm guessing tonight is going to prove that point.

"It's nothing to be ashamed of. I get it all the time. Put a little bit of this on it and it will be gone in a few days," Jenny says cheerfully.

Claire turns away from her and gives me *The Look*. The one that we silently give each other whenever our friend Jenny speaks. The one that quietly shouts "HOW THE FUCK DOES SHE FUNCTION ON A DAILY BASIS???"

"I'm pretty sure if Blistex was the cure for cancer, someone would have mentioned it by now, but thanks for the offer," Claire says with a chuckle as she sips her newly filled glass of wine.

"Oh, you said cancer! Ha! I totally thought you said canker. You know, like herpes, but on your lip... Oh. OH. OH, MY GOD!" Jenny screams in horror when it finally sinks in.

A few of the other patrons look our way when Jenny shouts and Claire gives them an apologetic look, waving them off with a flap of her hand.

Claire barely has time to set her wine glass down before Jenny flies out of her seat and tackles her in a bear hug.

"This can't be happening! You're so young. It's lung cancer, isn't it? I told you we never should have smoked all that pot in our twenties!" Jenny wails, burying her face in Claire's shoulder.

It's right around this point that I stop laughing. Not just because I can see it written all over Claire's face that I need to do something to get Jenny off of her because crying chicks and Claire do not mix, but because I can see it written all over Claire's face that she's not kidding. This isn't some weird April Fool's joke in the middle of July. She isn't going to shove Jenny away and shout, "Ha ha, you bunch of gullible assholes! I'm totally messing with you!"

While Jenny cries out her frustrations all over the shoulder of Claire's t-shirt, I do nothing but sit here staring at her. *I* should be the one crying. *I* should be the one running to the other side of the table hugging my best friend. *I* should be the one cursing God and shouting about the unfairness of it all. The problem is, I know exactly what I should be doing right now, but I can't make any of it happen. My ass has become permanently attached to the chair and my feet are like giant cement blocks refusing to move.

"Stop it," Claire says quietly, staring right at me as she pats Jenny's back.

I look at her in confusion.

"There is only one overly emotional woman in this group and that's how it's supposed to be. If you started crying right now I would punch you in the throat," Claire states softly.

And just like that, I'm reminded just how well she knows me. She knows I don't do the whole touchy-feely thing just like I know that in about three seconds, she's going to start getting the shakes from having Jenny's arms wrapped around her along with the sounds of female sobbing so close to her ear. There has to be something wrong with me though, right? I mean, my best friend has cancer.

My best friend has *cancer*.

Why can't I feel anything? Why can't I do anything?

Finally, Claire pulls herself out of Jenny's death grip and grabs a couple of napkins from the table, handing them to a still sniffling Jenny.

"I'm going to make this short and sweet. I found a lump in my breast last week and Carter made me immediately call my gynecologist. After I saw her, she sent me to an oncologist for a mammogram just to be on the safe side. I had a biopsy done and two days later the oncologist called to tell me I have breast cancer. I'm going in a week for a double mastectomy, and then I'll have six treatments of chemo and finally, reconstruction surgery. Now, back to my original question, who wants more wine?"

Jenny raises her hand. "I do!"

Claire lets out a cheer and unscrews the top on another bottle. We're such classy bitches.

"You know, Drew and I play mammogram all the time. I read about the importance of doing self-breast exams and of course Drew wanted to be helpful. He's so cute!"

Claire leans back against her chair as she shakes her head. "Do I even want to ask what exactly "playing mammogram" entails?"

"Well, Drew dresses up like a doctor and I put on a robe. Then, he takes two dinner plates from the kitchen and he smushes—"

"OKAY! Stop. That's enough. I'm going to puke up all this wine we've consumed. Never speak of that again. Ever," Claire warns her.

Reaching for the bottle Claire just opened, I opt out of pouring it into my glass and just chug it right from the bottle. Fuck it.

"Um, you can't do that."

With the bottle still close to my mouth, I turn to look at the judgmental waitress who is half my age.

"This is a bar," I tell her, holding the bottle of wine up in front of her face. "And THIS, is called alcohol. People like to drink it. IN A BAR."

The perky twenty-something puts her hands on her hips and glares at me. "You can't drink it straight out of the bottle."

"What are you, the wine police? Don't you have some Barbies that need to be played with somewhere?"

Jenny giggles, holding up her glass of wine. "Three cheers for Barbie! I learned what smithereens was with Gymnastics Barbie and Lifeguard Barbie."

"What the fuck is smithereens?" I ask, taking another swig from the bottle.

"You know, where two women lock their legs together and grind their hoo-has against each other," Jenny explains, making peace signs with both of her hands and then interlocking her fingers together.

"I think she means scissoring," Claire provides.

"Look, ma'am, I'm going to have to ask you to leave if you continue to drink out of the bottle," Slutty Waitress Barbie informs me.

"Awwwwww shit," Claire mutters as I slowly get out of my chair and stand in front of the girl.

"You did NOT just call me ma'am," I growl.

The waitress takes a step back and I feel good about the fact that even though I'm little, I'm mighty, and this bitch looks like she's afraid I'm going to punch her in the kidney.

"Steph, I promise I'll make sure she uses a glass," Claire tells the waitress kindly.

She smiles at Claire and nods. "Okay. Just, try not to

scream or cry anymore either. Some of the other customers are getting nervous."

I clunk the bottle of wine on the table and take a step in Steph's direction. "You should probably run along now before I find a fun way to make *you* scream and cry."

Steph *literally* runs away from our table and I sit back down, snatching the wine glass from Claire's hand that she is holding out for me.

"We should shave your head tonight," Jenny suddenly announces, bringing us all right back to the matter at hand that I DO NOT want to think about. "You have great bone structure. You'll look great with no hair."

"You are not shaving my head tonight. I don't start chemo for two weeks, so how about we just wait and see what happens?"

Jesus Christ. Mammogram. Lump. Biopsy. Mastectomy. Chemo. WHAT THE FUCK IS HAPPENING RIGHT NOW?

"And let me just add one last thing," Claire announces. "No one in this room will be shaving their head in support of me. There will be no spaghetti dinners to raise money for my medical costs, you are banned from wearing anything pink or anything closely related to the pink family until this is all over and there will be no fucking candlelight vigils held for me. Can I get an 'Amen' from both of you?"

"Amen!" I deadpan the reply and Jenny shouts it excitedly but hey, at least we replied.

Jenny starts talking Claire's ear off about her first mammogram last year and I stare into my glass of wine wondering when the fuck I'll wake up from this bullshit nightmare I'm obviously having. I mean, how is it possible that one of us is even old enough to get breast cancer? I'm not stupid, I've seen the statistics and I know it can hit anyone at any time, but those are people I don't know. They are women who have nothing to do with my life and I can continue living each day with only a passing thought about all of those poor ladies and what they're going through. A friend of a friend's mother's sister on Facebook, your mom's college roommate's aunt, your dentist's neighbor's best friend. THESE are the people who get cancer, not someone I know and love.

This is happening right in my own backyard. Right in our motherfucking favorite bar! It's impossible to stay oblivious anymore. Cancer has jumped off the pages of a Facebook post of a friend of a friend of a friend's yoga instructor's Starbuck's barista and smacked me right in the face.

Wasn't it just yesterday that Claire and I were in college, lamenting about her pesky virginity and dreaming about someday owning a business together?

Chapter 3

Sex and Cookies

Sophomore Year of College.
Still too many years ago to count…

"YOU GUYS! THERE'S a party at Pi Kappa Phi tonight!
You absolutely HAVE to go!"

Claire and I glanced up from our spot on the floor of
our dorm room where we'd been looking through our pile
of VHS movies trying to decide if it was a *Girls Just Want
to Have Fun* or *The Lost Boys* kind of night. We tried not to
groan when we saw Candy standing in the doorway.

After years of us telling her point blank to her
face that she was entirely too fucking chipper to be
friends with us, she still hadn't gotten the hint. Imagine
our surprise when she enrolled in the same college as us

two years ago and made sure we all lived in the same dorm.

"Wow, that sounds like a blast, but we have a project due on Monday testing the abhorrent amount of genetic mutations in certain female subjects with ecdysiast-related given names. Sorry," Claire told her with a shrug.

Candy stared at her in confusion for a few seconds before rolling her eyes and giggling. "I swear, one of these days I'm going to get you two to go to a Pi Kappa Phi frat party and it's going to change your lives."

"Yeah, that will be the day," Claire muttered under her breath as Candy blew us kisses and ran down the hall, shouting in excitement to a few poor souls who happened to be in her frat-party warpath.

"Remind me again why we didn't get an apartment off campus and away from that fuck-knob?" Claire asked.

"Because we're trying to be economical and save money for the sex club that we're going to open as soon as we graduate," I reminded her. "Also, ecdysiast-related given names?"

I raised my eyebrow at Claire as she pushed herself up from the floor and sat down on the bottom bunk.

"Ecdysiast means striptease performer. It was on my word-of-the-day calendar yesterday," Claire explained before she flopped onto her back. "Also, we're not opening a sex club. That's just gross."

Pushing the movies aside, I got up from the floor and

joined her on the bed. We lie next to each other in silence, staring up at the wooden slats under my top bunk that I'd decorated with bumper stickers:

What's your damage, Heather?

CORN NUTS!

Does Barry Manilow know that you raid his wardrobe?

What's that smell? Vampires, my friend. Vampires.

It's called a sense of humor.

You should get one, they're nice.

My Little Pony: Friendship is Magic

Where in the fuck did that MLP one come from?

"Do you think there's something wrong with us because we don't like people?" I asked Claire after a few minutes. I reached up and used my fingernail to start picking at the edge of that stupid My Little Pony sticker.

Claire grabbed my wrist and pulled it away. "Don't take that one down, I like it!"

"Seriously? My Little Pony? What are we, ten?"

Claire shrugged, sliding her hands behind her head. "I have a feeling they're going to make a comeback someday. Leave MLP alone."

With an irritated scowl, I rolled onto my side to face her. "So, seriously. Are we weird?"

Claire turned her head to face me. "No, we aren't weird. We just have a low tolerance for bullshit. Who cares if we haven't gone to a Pi Kappa Phi party yet and made out with random douchebags? I mean really, those parties are crawling with STDs. You could probably get knocked up just by ringing the doorbell."

We both laughed at that thought and then it got quiet again.

Even though we'd been to plenty of frat parties during our two years of college, we'd avoided Pi Kappa like the plague. That was the house known for its jocks and snotty rich boys. It was also the house that threw the best fucking parties on the planet, though, and pretty much everyone at this school and every school within a seventy-five mile radius showed up. Except for Claire and I.

"Do YOU feel like we're weird because we haven't been to one yet? I mean, if that's the case, I would totally suffer through a Pi Kappa party to make you happy," Claire informed me. "Just because it isn't my idea of fun, doesn't mean it's not yours. Who knows? You could meet the love of your life there."

Claire moved her hands under her chin and fluttered her eyelashes at me. "Oh, you big, strong, frat boy! Please, do another keg stand to pledge your undying love for me!"

I punched her in the arm as I laughed. "Oh, shut up, you whore. I'm pretty sure I won't meet the love of my life or even someone worth a one-night stand at one of those things, but it might be nice to check one out and see what all the fuss is about. I mean, this is our sophomore year. We should do something memorable."

Claire looked at me in mock horror. "Oh, my God! You mean watching movies or going to the boring frat parties where they serve h'orderves and cups of tea every Friday night while we smuggle in Boone's Farm in our purses isn't memorable?"

Speaking of Boone's Farm...

I quickly scrambled off the bed and pulled two bottles of Boone's Farm Strawberry Hill out from under the bed and held them up.

Claire immediately started laughing, sprang forward and grabbed one of the bottles out of my hand and unscrewed the top. "Jesus, we're so fucking classy. It doesn't get much better than screw-tops."

She chugged a good amount of wine before letting out a loud, satisfied sigh and lying back down, resting the bottle on her stomach. I set the unopened bottle next to me in bed before grabbing Claire's and taking a sip.

"Okay, so frat parties aside, we should really talk about the sex club," I told her.

"You're going to have to ply me with something a hell of a lot stronger than wine with only four percent alcohol in it to get me to agree to that shit," Claire informed me, snatching the bottle back and taking another sip.

"Fine, it doesn't have to be JUST a sex club. Maybe we could pair it with something you're interested in. Make it sort of a joint company. What are you interested in, Claire?"

She thought about it for a minute while I curled up next to her and we passed the bottle of shitty but delicious wine back and forth.

"It would probably be easier to tell you what I'm not interested in. Like say, a club where people are doing gross things to each other in public," she told me, sticking her finger in her mouth and mock-gagging.

"You are such a fucking buzz kill. Fine. We can rethink the sex club aspect, but we WILL own a business together. Maybe if you'd finally give it up to someone, Virgin McVirginsen, you would be more agreeable to all things involving sex," I reminded her.

The virgin comment was Claire's cue to punch me in the arm. I loved this girl to death, but she was wound up entirely too tight, pun motherfucking intended. I'd been trying to convince her to get rid of that pesky virginity since high school, but she was dead set on finding "the one." She didn't need to find "the one." She just needed to find the one who would do for a few hours. Scratch that, we're talking college boys. A few minutes, tops.

"Stop talking out of your ass. I'll show you. Maybe I'll drag you to one of those stupid frat parties and have a one-night stand," Claire threatened.

I started laughing. And once I started I couldn't stop.

"Shut up! It could totally happen!" Claire argued.

"Right! It will happen just like My Little Pony will

make a comeback. Give it a rest, Claire. You're not the one-night-stand type and that's perfectly okay. One slut in a friendship is one slut too many."

Claire shook her head at me. "You're not a slut. You're just equal opportunity. You buy eight pairs of shoes at one time because you can't stand the idea of leaving a pair in the store to get lonely. It's only natural you do the same with your vagina. You never want your vagina to be lonely. It's so beautiful."

I chugged half the bottle of Boone's while Claire laughed.

"Okay, in all seriousness, I really want to own a bakery some day. What if we sold like sexy lingerie on one side and cookies and cupcakes on the other?" she suggested.

I started to make fun of the idea, but then I thought about it. And thought about it some more. I thought about it while I polished off the rest of the bottle and then chucked the empty onto the floor.

"Heeeeey, wine whore!" Claire complained as I jumped up from the bed and started pacing the room.

"Sex and cookies," I muttered.

Claire paused in the process of opening the second bottle of wine. "Huh?"

"Sex and cookies. Oh, fuck, Claire! You're a GENIUS!" I shouted.

"Wait. Let me drink some of this and catch up to you before you shower me with more compliments."

She held her hand up in the air in the universal sign of "hold the fuck up" while she downed half the bottle. She wiped her arm across her mouth and belched loudly. "Okay, I'm ready. Tell me more. Make sure to add how pretty and nice I am."

I walked over to my desk and sat down, grabbing a pen and a notebook. I wrote "Sex and Cookies" really big at the top of a blank page.

"So, I like sex and you like baking. Jesus, this is brilliant. BRILLIANT!" I screamed as I made a list of things we could sell at this store and a rough estimate of how much money it would take to get something like this off the ground. Turns out my Business Administration classes were actually useful. Who knew?

"Fuck. They put more than four percent alcohol in this shit. I think I'm drunk," Claire mumbled as she squinted her eyes and tried to read the label on the bottle.

"Nah, I just roofied you."

Claire sniffed the opening of the bottle and then shrugged. "Cool. Make sure you take advantage of me when I pass out. Anyway, back to this Snack and Sex thing. Tell me more."

I scribbled a few more things on the paper before turning the chair to face her. "Sex and Cookies, asshole. It's the name of our future business endeavor, although we might have to tweak that a little. I'm not sure the city would allow us to put the word 'sex' on our sign, but whatever. You can have your bakery on one side and put people into sugar comas every day and I can sell sex toys and lingerie and shit like that and put people into erotic comas on my side. Then, we can make sure the building has a loft upstairs and live above our businesses and throw awesome parties every weekend. WINNER!" I shouted.

Claire bolted forward on the bed so fast she smacked her head into the wooden slats of the top bunk.

"SON OF A BITCH!" she yelled, rubbing her hand on her head as she got up and walked over to me.

I got up from the chair and we stood staring at each other for a few minutes before both of our faces broke out into huge smiles. We grabbed onto each other and started screaming and laughing and jumping up and down in the middle of the room like a couple of assholes.

After we got that nonsense out of our system, we went to work making more lists.

"This is totally happening. We'll go to a Pi Kappa Phi party next weekend and make THAT dream come true, and then right after graduation in two years, we're opening this fucking business!" Claire stated.

We finished off the second bottle of Boone's Farm in celebration and popped our worn out copy of *Heathers* into the VCR on the dresser, reciting the words to the entire movie while we dreamed about our awesome future.

Chapter 4

Hello, My Name is Zoltron

I STOOD IN the corner of the room, staring at Claire and thinking about the day we came up with the idea for Seduction and Snacks as the nurse got her IV started. She doesn't look sick. How in the fuck is this happening? Sure, we're in our mid-forties, but we're still young. This does NOT happen to young people and it most certainly doesn't happen to one of MY people.

She met my eyes across the room and huffed. "Will you stop looking at me like that?"

"Like what?" I ask, pushing away from the wall and going to the edge of the bed.

"Like you're expecting me to start spewing green vomit or keel over."

I scoff and put my hands on my hips. "That's not funny. This is serious, Claire. You... you're..."

"I have breast cancer. It's okay, you can say it. My tits may be small, but they're deadly," she says with a laugh.

"The doctor just gave me this form she says you need to fill out," Drew interrupts, walking through the door.

For the first time since I met him, I'm actually glad to see Drew. Ever since Claire told us the news and we almost got kicked out of Fosters, he's been the calm, rational one. We met Drew when Claire met her husband, Carter. Drew and Carter had just recently moved to our town and they worked at the same car manufacturing plant where my husband Jim worked. From day one, Drew was always the guy who said whatever he was thinking no matter how inappropriate or disgusting it was. He's the jokester in the group, the crazy dude you sometimes don't want to be seen in public with. Who am I kidding? You never want to be seen in public with Drew. The last few days, though, he's kept us all from falling apart and on a few occasions, I've actually thought about hugging him to thank him. Then I remember the story he told us last week about how he and his wife Jenny decided Tuesdays were now referred to as Taco Tuesday in their house. Something to do with salsa on his penis and Jenny wearing a sombrero. I've blocked out the rest of that story out of respect for my mental health.

"What's the form for?" Claire asks, craning her neck

to look at the paper Drew holds out to her.

"It's all about your likes and dislikes and some 'getting to know you' shit. It's like the cancer version of Match.com. I think they want you to get a little action while you're here," Drew replies.

The nurse finishes up Claire's IV and smiles at us. "That's just a way for the staff to get to learn a little more about you. We want you to be as comfortable as possible and we feel that knowing some personal things about you helps us make that easier."

She fiddles with the IV machine, presses a few buttons and then leaves the room, telling Claire she'll be back in a little while to check on her and pick up the finished form.

"I don't have the energy to fill that thing out, will you guys do it for me?" Claire asks, closing her eyes and resting her head on the pillow behind her.

At this point, I would strip naked, light myself on fire and run screaming through the halls of this hospital if she asked. It's not easy for someone like me to feel helpless. I've spent my life being known as the bossy, take-charge one in this group. Having to stand off to the side and watch your person suffering and not being able to do a damn thing about it is sobering.

"Don't you worry your pretty little head, Claire. Jim and I will fill this out for you," Drew announces with a smile as my husband and Carter walk through the door, their arms loaded with coffee, bags of chips, Snickers,

Pepsi and anything else they could find in the vending machine down the hall.

"Dude, they had pudding cups in the vending machine?" Drew asks, his eyes growing wide as he snatches a chocolate cup out of Carter's hand.

"Uh, not exactly. We found a fridge a few doors down and it was filled with a bunch of free stuff!" Jim explains.

I shake my head at them. "You guys, that's probably the nurse's lounge. You just stole someone's lunch."

Drew already has the top off of the pudding cup and we all watch as he reaches into the pocket of his jeans and pulls out a mini bottle of Kahlua. He unscrews the top and dumps the entire thing into the cup of pudding, using his fingers to stir the mixture around.

"Mmmmmm pudding shots," he mutters before tipping the cup back and slurping the entire thing down in one gulp.

Carter busies himself dumping all of the food on a table in the corner of the room, lining it up by size and then rearranging it by color. He huffs and then tries organizing the items alphabetically. Carter has been manically arranging things since Claire got the call from her oncologist last week. He started at Seduction and Snacks, putting all of the butt plugs with the ball gags because they both start with B. After that, he took every item out of their pantry at home and lined them up by expiration date. When he tried to rearrange Claire's baking cupboards, that's when she put her foot down and told him if he put the cinnamon near the coriander she would castrate him.

I feel for the guy, I really do. He needs to keep himself busy so he doesn't dwell on what's happening with Claire. I tried doing something like that after she told us. I decided it was a good idea to take up running. Jim found me an hour later, two blocks away from our house screaming about how no one in their right mind should run unless someone with a gun was chasing them. Even then, I might just let the guy shoot me. Running is dumb.

"Carter, stop diddling the applesauce cups and come help us fill out this form," Drew tells him, waving the piece of paper up in the air. "I have more yummy goodness in my pants and pudding cups to fill."

"Oh, Jesus," Jim mutters next to me. Still, it doesn't deter him from going over to Drew, grabbing one of the pudding cups and an offered mini bottle of vodka that Drew just pulled out of his back pocket.

I watch as Carter goes over to Claire's side, leans down and whispers something in her ear before kissing her on the head and disappearing out the door with Jim and Drew. This is the first time the two of us have been alone since we all got the news. It's also the first time I have no idea what to say to my best friend. Everything that runs through my mind right now is completely stupid.

"So, this kind of sucks, huh?"

"At least your oncologist is cute."

"Would it be wrong to ask if they have some extra morphine I can use?"

"Sorry if I can't stop staring at your boobs."

"Stop staring at my boobs," Claire deadpans, her eyes still closed on the pillow.

"How the hell did you know I was staring at your boobs?"

She opens her eyes and raises one brow at me. "Because the lump in there has a special homing beacon that can sense boob ogling."

I cross my arms over my chest and roll my eyes. "You are being entirely too flippant about all of this."

"What do you expect me to do, Liz? Scream and cry about the unfairness of it all? What good will that do me? Do you think the cancer will be like 'Well, shit. If she thinks it's unfair then we obviously need to skedaddle.'"

"Did you just say *skedaddle*?"

Claire nods her head. "Yes, yes I did. Now quit being a pussy, come over here and sit by me."

She pats the bed next to her. "It's not contagious."

"I know it's not contagious, asshole," I tell her as I gently climb into her bed and lean back against the pillows next to her.

We don't say anything, each of us staring up at the ceiling. I want to tell her how sorry I am, but that's so fucking cliché that I can't even form the words. I want to reassure her that whatever she needs, I'll be here for her, but what the hell could I give her right now to make this all better? I don't have a magic wand that will take this stupid fucking disease out of her body. In less than an hour, she's going into an operating room to have a double mastectomy for stage 2 breast cancer. I have nothing that will make any of this go away.

A half hour later, the boys walk back into the room, snickering and shoving each other, clearly a little tipsy from pudding shots.

"What did you guys do? How many of those cups of pudding did you have?" Claire questions.

"I have no idea what you're talking about, Zoltron," Jim replies with a laugh.

Drew chokes on his own laugh, bending over at the waist.

"Zoltron? Do I even want to know what you three idiots are talking about?" I ask as Jim walks over and hands me the questionnaire the nurse asked Claire to fill out.

I grab it from his hand and scroll through the questions, along with the answers the boys filled in.

"Question number one: Do you have any nicknames?" I read aloud.

Claire leans forward to look over my shoulder, reading the answer that they wrote down. "My full name is Sheba, Princess of the Night, but I will only answer to Zoltron."

The boys start giggling like fools from the doorway.

"Keep going," Drew says in between laughs.

I sigh, moving on to question number two. "Do you have any hobbies?"

I feel Claire's rumble of laughter next to me as she reads the answer. "My hobbies include running a meth lab in my basement, throwing down gang signs, mailing underwear to members of Congress and breeding ferrets."

I quickly scan the rest of the questions and answers.

• **What is your favorite color?** Clitoris. A combination of clear, teal, orange and island blue.

• **What is your favorite song?** The Silent Song. I could sing it for you, but you wouldn't be able to hear it. Only alpacas and very rare mice have the ability to hear The Silent Song.

• **Do you have any children?** rufus, joseephus, artie choke, woody bush, pat may wiener, meowy, boopsie and bob.

- **What's your favorite movie?** It's a tie between "The Anal girls of tobacco road: vagina slimes" and "sex starved fuck sluts #22: stinky white women." The well-developed plot and range of emotions portrayed in vagina slimes far outweighs that of stinky white women, but at the same time, the complexity in the cinematic quality of stinky white women should not be overlooked.

The questionnaire goes on for two pages, each answer they wrote down worse than the last. The only thing stopping me from throttling the idiot men we married is the fact that Claire thinks it's funny and it's taken her mind off of the fact that her boobs are killing her. Those little bumps of fat sitting on her chest are literally sucking the life out of her. I keep running through every single memory of the two of us together. Every time we've made each other laugh, cry, snort, puke, trip down stairs or scream in frustration. Thirty years of going through everything together. I can't imagine living the rest of my life without her and I have no idea how to find the humor in any of this bullshit. We have so much more living to do, she and I. We have a business to run together, the wedding of our children to plan and future grandchildren to corrupt.

The nurse walks back in to grab the form, clearly irritated that there are three drunk men giggling like little girls in the room, trying on hospital masks that they drew smiley faces on the front of.

"There's no drinking of alcohol allowed on hospital premises," she tells them haughtily.

"Pudding shots do not equal drinking alcohol," Drew informs her, his voice muffled through the hospital mask that has a porn stache drawn on the front of it. "Pudding shots equal awesome. Can I call you 'Puddin'?"

"I'm going to have to ask you to leave," she tells him.

He throws his arm around her shoulders. "Awwww, don't be like that, Puddin. We'll share some with you."

As I wrangle the guys and get them out of the room to give Claire some peace and quiet and get Nurse Ratched off our backs, I suddenly wish I could turn back time. I'd go back to something better than this. A time when my best friend wasn't getting ready to go into surgery so they could try and cut out the part of her body that's killing her. A time when I was young and dumb. Those were the good old days...

Chapter 5

Non One-Night Stand

HERE'S A LITTLE secret that not too many people know: Claire wasn't the only one who had a one-night stand that one time at a frat party. Unlike my dumbass friend, at least I remembered the birth control and didn't get knocked up. Well, birth control that works. I guess it isn't her fault condoms break every once in a while.

That one time, at a frat party…

CLAIRE HAD DISAPPEARED with some really cute guy about twenty minutes ago and honestly, I was glad she walked out of the room. The two of them were trading lines from *Heathers* while they played a thousand games of beer pong and it had started making me feel stabby.

Heathers was our thing. OURS. Now that whore decided to finally listen to me about losing her virginity with a dude who was going to steal her away from me. Some pretty boy with a sweet smile who was going to pop her cherry, ask her to marry him and then they would move away and I'd never see her again. Okay, I know I'm being dramatic, fuck your face. I'm a good friend, though. I stood watch over the guy all night long and made sure he wasn't some pompous frat boy who would slip a roofie in her drink and take advantage of her. The fact that he was actually *nice* made it harder to hate him for stealing my best friend. Thank God Claire strapped on a set of balls and took the lead, otherwise that guy would have just stared at her with those stupid googly eyes all night long and never manned up. That guy was two seconds away from kissing the ground she walked on. Really, I'm happy for her. If she's going to lose her virginity, at least it's with someone like that and not some douche who will hit it and quit it and she'll never see him again. I hope she at least remembers to get his damn name.

"You look bored. How can you possibly be bored at a frat party?"

I turned around so fast when I heard a voice close to my ear that my full cup of beer sloshed all down the front of the guy's clothes.

He let out a yell when the cold liquid hit his junk and I growled when I realized I'd just wasted a full cup of perfectly good beer. As he attempted to pull his wet shirt away from his body, I looked over at the keg that now had a red Solo cup covering the tap indicating it was empty.

Super. Just perfect. I have to stand here and wait for my best friend to finish doing the deed sober.

I started to move towards the kitchen in the hopes of finding something, *anything* to drink when a hand grabbed onto my arm. I had really good intentions, I swear. My mouth opened and I prepared to let a string of curse words fly, telling this asshole to get his hands off me before I kicked him in the balls, but my eyes met his and I forgot how to swear. I don't forget how to swear. I NEVER forget how to swear. Swearing is my favorite thing in the world and I always have some good ones on the tip of my tongue ready to fly just in case. Hazel eyes with a ring of green around them stared down at me and I swear to fuck they sparkled as he looked at me. Gorgeous eyes aside, the guy had the nerve to smile at me. Not smirk like a douche, but a full, showing all his teeth and the dimples in his cheeks *smile*.

"I promise I won't say something stupid like 'How about you help me get out of these wet clothes,' but… I really need to get out of these wet clothes," he told me.

I just stood there staring at his lips as he spoke.

"I have an extra t-shirt and jeans out in my car, but I'm afraid if I go out and get them, you won't be here when I get back."

Finally, I tore my eyes away from his mouth and

shook the cobwebs from my brain. I took a step back from him, putting some distance between us before I did something stupid like kiss the guy.

"What do you care if I'm not here when you get back? There are a hundred girls at this party," I replied lamely.

He shrugged. "You're the only one who looks like she doesn't want to be here and that intrigues me. It also doesn't hurt that you're the prettiest girl I've ever seen."

My mouth dropped open unattractively and I'm pretty sure he wanted to take that statement back immediately. I've been called hot, sexy, gorgeous and a bunch of other adjectives that I couldn't have cared less about, but no one had ever told me I was pretty. That word indicates sweet and nice and innocent—something I had never been. It also made my heart melt, which pissed me off. My heart never melts.

"My name is Jim," he told me with that fucking smile again.

He held his hand out in front of him and there was nothing I could do but take it. I mean, I didn't want the poor guy looking like a schmuck with his hand hanging there while I stared him down.

You know in all those romance novels how people feel 'sparks' the first time they touch? Yeah, totally stupid. And no, I didn't feel fucking sparks. Jim isn't a lightning rod and last time I checked I didn't have an electrical plug coming out of my ass connected to an outlet in the wall. I felt soft, warm skin and a hand that engulfed my small one and held on tight. I felt his handshake all the way up my arms and somewhere in my vagina. He held my hand and didn't let go even after the two second time limit for proper handshakes ended.

"I'm not having sex with you tonight," I blurted.

He squeezed my hand and leaned in close, his cheek brushing against mine until his lips were right by my ear.

"What makes you think I *want* to have sex with you?"

I should have been offended by his words, but I wasn't because I actually believed him. He seriously did NOT want to have sex with me. It was an anomaly and it made me want to know more about him. He pulled away from me and dropped my hand, sticking his own hands into the front pockets of his jeans.

"Look, I'm not into one-night stands. Sure, they're fun at the time but the next morning, you always wake up feeling used."

He started backing away from me, pushing his way through crowds of drunk college students.

"Besides, I don't even know your name!" he shouted before disappearing behind two drunk girls dry humping each other while a group of equally drunk guys cheered them on.

I looked behind me down the hall where Claire had disappeared, and then I stared off in the general direction of where Jim had been swallowed up by the group of idiots. Back and forth I looked, trying to decide which way to go. I know I should have ran down the hall and stood guard outside of the room Claire entered with Mr. Cherry Popper, but the thought of *listening* to what was going on behind that closed door made me want to throw up all the beer I'd consumed tonight. If I followed Jim out to his car while he got his change of clothes, I'd have to give him my name and actually *talk* to him. What he said about one-night stands was obviously true, but at least they were quick and painless. You found a guy, you had sex and then you went on your merry way and didn't have to deal with all the baggage and bullshit. In the end, I made the only choice I *could* make. I tossed my empty beer cup onto the ground and pushed the dry-humpers out of the way, running outside to try and find Jim and see what his deal was.

After ten minutes of jogging up and down the block, searching row after row of cars parked bumper to bumper for the party, I located Jim. He'd already changed into dry jeans and was in the process of pulling off his wet shirt.

I stopped at the front of his car and stared at his bare chest. I'm a sucker for muscular men. Give me a big, hulking beast of a man who can toss me over their shoulder any day. Jim wouldn't be cracking any walnuts with the sheer power of his biceps anytime soon, but he was in great shape. He was tall and lean and had a six-pack I wanted to run my fingers over. I may or may not have let out a whimper when he grabbed his clean shirt from the backseat and covered himself up.

He spotted me as soon as he got the shirt pulled down and that damn smile lit up his face again. I was going to swoon like those motherfuckers in romance novels. My legs were going to give out and I'd need smelling salts or some shit.

"So, before we get out of here and get some coffee, do you think I could get your name?" he asked as he closed his back door and walked up to me.

"Liz, my name is Liz. Just coffee, right?"

He nodded as he grabbed my hand and laced his fingers through mine.

"Yep, just coffee. I know a great place two blocks from here."

And that's how it all started. We walked to the coffee shop and spent three hours talking before heading to Jim's apartment and having the most amazing sex of my life. True to his word, though, Jim didn't do one-night stands. When I woke up the next morning and tried to quietly pull the covers back and sneak out, he jumped out of bed and started getting dressed.

"Are you hungry? I'm starving. The diner across the street makes the best pancakes. Breakfast is on me and then we can figure out what to do the rest of the day."

Normally, I would have found his assertiveness off-putting and told him to suck it, but I couldn't. I was fucking starving and the thought of a huge plate piled with pancakes made my mouth water. He held my hand the whole walk down two flights of stairs and across the street to the diner. When he excused himself to go to the bathroom after we ordered, he came over to my side of the table and kissed the top of my head. Over breakfast, we made plans to spend the rest of the day together taking a nap and watching movies. I eagerly arranged these things with him and didn't even realize what was happening. I was falling in love with a guy I just met. A guy who held open doors, pulled out my chair, asked me about myself and my dreams and refused to let our night together be something cheap.

I haven't spent more than a few nights apart from Jim in over twenty years and it's mostly thanks to Claire. After our day of cuddling and watching movies, I swear to God I started to break out in hives. I'd never had a relationship. I didn't know the first thing about spending more than a few hours with a guy. What in the hell would we even talk about? He'd get bored with me and walk away right when I got attached. I snuck into the bathroom during our movie marathon and made a frantic call to Claire. She told me to stop being an asshole and give him a chance to prove me wrong.

And prove me wrong he did. It was the best non-one-night stand I'd ever had. He tells me when I'm being an asshole and I tell him when he's pissing me off. He's my rock and he keeps me grounded. Aside from Claire, he's the only person who knows just by looking at me what

I'm feeling. Sometimes it's a blessing, but with everything going on right now, it's a fucking curse.

Chapter 6

Shaved Pussy

As SOON AS the doctor came out and told us that Claire's surgery went well and that she was resting comfortably, I left. Shitty thing to do, I know, but I couldn't take it anymore. I couldn't stand to drink one more cup of shitty hospital coffee and I was losing my mind pacing the shitty halls. I told everyone I was going to pick up some food so we didn't have to eat one more shitty meal in the cafeteria, grabbed the keys from Jim and ran to the parking garage. I've done nothing but drive around for an hour. I drove past Seduction and Snacks where we made our dreams come true, the park where Claire and I used to take the kids when they were little, the elementary school where we both got kicked out of the PTA for rolling our eyes at the president when she told us we needed to be more bubbly to be in the Parent Teacher Association, the high school where we met and then later sent our own kids, and finally, the hotel where Gavin and Charlotte had decided to have their wedding reception in six months.

Our kids are getting married, something we used to talk about when they were babies and it's actually happening. We've been fighting over what color dresses we're going to wear and who's going to cater the event and what song would be the perfect one to dance to when it comes time for the mother/daughter, mother/son dance. All the years of dreaming, all these months of planning and arguing and now I don't know if my best friend will even be there when our children tie the knot. There hasn't been one major event in my life that Claire hasn't been there for and now, the biggest one of all is coming and I might have to do it on my own. It's not fair. I can't do this without her. I can't do *anything* without her.

Before I head back to the hospital, I decide to stop by Claire's house and pick up a few things that she might need. I'm sure Carter packed everything in her closet, but I'm not ready to go back to the hospital just yet. I need some time to get my head on straight so I don't break down crying as soon as I walk into her room.

Pulling into the driveway, I see Carter's car parked in front of the garage and wonder what he's doing home. Figuring he had the same idea as me, I let myself into the house to look for him. When I get close to the kitchen, a can of green beans comes flying out into the hallway, denting the wall right next to my head. Crouching down, I peek around the kitchen doorway right as Carter reaches into the pantry and swipes his arm across every single shelf, sending cans of soup, boxes of Mac N Cheese, canisters of sugar and about a hundred other things crashing to the floor. When the pantry is empty, he moves on to the cabinets, yanking out pots and pans and tossing them across the room. Pans crash into the table, lids smack into the wall and he kicks a bag of flour out of his way as he moves across the room to wreak havoc on the cupboards under the island. Unfortunately, the toe of his shoe hits the bag of flour just right and the entire thing explodes, a cloud of white powder *poofing* all over the floor and the front of his jeans.

"MOTHERFUCKER!" he screams.

I've never seen Carter like this and for a minute, I'm afraid to approach him. I quickly pull out my phone and send a text to Jim and Drew, hoping they can get their asses over here and help me out.

Carter sees me cowering in the doorway and stalks over to me as I shove my phone in my pocket.

"I don't know what the fuck to do," he tells me angrily before turning and slamming his foot into a Tupperware dish, sending it flying across the room.

"I DON'T KNOW WHAT THE FUCK TO DO!" he screams.

He clutches his hands in his hair and I'm frozen in

place as I watch him sink to the ground on his knees in the middle of the mess.

"FUCK YOU, GOD! FUCK YOU FOR DOING THIS TO HER!" he cries, his shoulders shaking with sobs as he completely breaks down.

I force myself to move, stepping over cans and boxes as I rush to his side and get down on my knees next to him, wrapping my arms around his heaving shoulders.

"This isn't fair! Goddammit, this isn't fair," he tells me angrily.

His entire body is shaking and for the first time since I found out about Claire being sick, I don't feel so helpless and alone. All this time, Carter has been a rock for Claire, doing whatever she needed and taking care of things when rage and fear were bubbling just under the surface. We share a love for Claire that is different in a lot of ways, but so alike in others. She is our soul mate and we are both caught in the middle of wanting to do everything we can to make her better, yet knowing there's not a damn thing we can do.

"I can't do this without her, Liz, I can't. Every part of my life is wrapped up in her. She's my wife, the mother of my children and my *everything*. How am I supposed to live without her?" he sobs.

I don't know how to answer him because everything I can think to say would be so fucking cliché. *She's going to be fine. You aren't going to lose her. She's strong and she's going to fight this.*

It's all bullshit. All of it. We *want* her to be fine. We *want* her to be with us forever, but that doesn't mean it's going to happen. How do you prepare yourself for a life without your soul mate, while at the same time holding onto hope that they will be okay? You have to walk a fine line between hope and reality, and every single day that line gets thinner and thinner. Eventually, you're going to have to tip one way or another and you have no way of knowing which way it will be. It's enough to drive you insane, to push you over the edge and make you question everything you thought you knew about yourself as a person.

"I'm so scared, Carter," I tell him honestly.

"I know, babe. Me too."

He keeps his arm slung over my shoulder as we move to the wall, resting our backs against it as we sit side-by-side with our knees pulled up to our chests. I can see some relief in Carter's face as we sit here in silence. It's like he just needed to scream and rage and get it out of his system in order to feel normal again. I wish I could do the same. No amount of trashing a kitchen is going to make me feel better, though.

I hear the front door open and shut and a few seconds later, Jim and Drew stick their heads in the kitchen, staring wide-eyed at the mess.

"Dude, have you been snorting cocaine without me?" Drew asks as he eyes the flour coating Carter's jeans.

"Why are you wearing shorts? Last time I checked it

was twenty degrees outside," Carter asks him.

Drew waltzes up to us and sticks one of his legs in front of Carter. "Touch it. Go ahead, touch it."

Carter shakes his head back and forth and tries to move away from Drew's leg. Drew just sticks his leg closer to Carter's face until it's practically touching his mouth.

"TOUCH IT!" Drew shouts.

"What the fuck is wrong with you?! I'm not touching your leg!" Carter argues.

Drew bends over, running his hand up and down his leg and I swear I hear him purr. "Oh, yeah, silky smooth."

"What in the hell is happening right now?" I ask Jim, who's standing right behind Drew, shaking his head.

"Our friend decided to shave his legs in support of Claire. Don't ask," Jim tells me.

"I totally get why chicks do this," Drew mutters. "I can't stop touching myself."

"Please tell me you didn't shave *your* legs," I tell my husband.

He sits down next to me on the floor and shrugs. "Nah, my legs are still hairy. My balls on the other hand…"

"You shaved your balls?" Carter asks, leaning forward to look at Jim.

Drew nods, his hands still running up and down his leg. "Yep, Jimbo totally shaved his nut sack. His bathroom now looks like someone killed Sasquatch. You know, if Sasquatch was covered in pube hair."

"Uh, did you guys do this together or something?" I ask in disgust.

"Are you kidding? That would be totally gay," Drew scoffs.

"And shaving your legs isn't?"

He just shrugs. "I figured we should do something in honor of Claire and I also heard that you can donate your hair to cancer patients so they can make wigs out of it. How cool would it be if someone was wearing my leg hair on their head?"

"That is the most disgusting thing I have ever heard. You can't donate leg hair, idiot," I tell him.

"Why the fuck not? I'll have you know my leg hair was long and flowing. It would make a beautiful wig."

Carter laughs and even though the idiot I married and his friend are morons, at least they managed to make Carter laugh, which is exactly what I'd hoped for when I sent them a text.

"Don't laugh, dude. It's your turn now," Jim states.

"I'm not shaving my legs and for your information, my balls have been silky smooth for years," Carter informs them.

"Oh, you're not going to shave anything on *your* body," Drew says with a smile, pulling a pair of battery operated clippers from his back pocket. "Find your pussy."

Carter and I look at Drew in confusion until a few

seconds later we hear a small "meow" from the corner of the room and Drew's face lights up with a huge smile.

"No. Absolutely not. You are NOT shaving Claire's cat," I tell them.

The guys sit perfectly still, looking back and forth between each other and I have a moment of hope that Drew was just kidding and that my husband and Carter aren't stupid enough to do something like this.

My hope is short lived, though. The poor cat lets out another "meow" and all three guys scramble up off the floor, shoving and pushing each other out of the way as they chase the cat through the house. Figuring there's no point in chasing after those morons, I start cleaning up the kitchen while listening to the guys screaming and laughing all through the house. Eventually, I hear the *whirr* of the clippers starting up and Drew lets out a war cry. "LONG LIVE SHAVED PUSSY!"

Thank God for good friends. Even though they have brains the size of peas, at least they got Carter's mind off of things for a few seconds. I wish the same could be said for me. I wish I could let my friends distract me and remember all the other stupid, silly things we've done together, instead of the sadness that is consuming our lives right now. I wish I could go back to a time when I actually knew how to make things better for my best friend.

Chapter 7

Cow Ass

Twenty-five years and nine months ago…
D-Day. Or is it P-Day?

"Remind me again why we decided to major in business? This business math bullshit is for the birds," I complained as I walked into our dorm room and tossed my backpack on my bunk. "Someone needs to get it through these professors' heads that we will NEVER need to use algebra to find X at any time other than in college. X can go fuck himself right in the face if he gets lost or can't figure out who he is."

When Claire didn't immediately reply back with an "Amen, sister!" I knew something was wrong. I saw her car parked downstairs, so I was pretty certain she was here. I'd been a shitty friend lately, not spending enough time with her since Jim decided to fuck with my head and my heart and I happily went along for the ride. I finally put my foot down today and told him I needed to spend some time with my girl. She'd been acting weird the last few weeks and I didn't like it.

"Claire?" I yelled as took off my coat and tossed it on top of my backpack.

I heard a sniffle come from the tiny bathroom in our dorm room. Pushing the door open, I found her sitting on the shitty yellow tile, surrounded by pregnancy tests with tears and snot running down her face.

"What's going on? Is this some kind of experiment for one of your classes?" I asked dumbly.

"I drank an entire gallon of milk in less than three minutes and did you know cows don't take pregnancy tests? A farmer sticks his hand up a cow's ass and feels around for a little ball of baby cow in her uterus. You have no idea how glad I am that I'm not a cow. No one needs to be up to their elbows in my anus," Claire rambled as she wiped the tears from her face.

"What in the actual fuck are you talking about right now?" I asked in horror, trying to get the image of an entire human arm shoved up a cow's ass out of my head.

"No need to fear, pasteurization does NOT mess with the hormone called human chorionic gonadotropin, or in layman's terms, HCG. This hormone is produced right after a fertilized egg attaches to the wall of a woman's uterus and OH, MY GOD I feel like I'm in fifth grade health class all over again and I WANT TO DIE!" she wailed as a fresh set of tears started pouring from her eyes.

Kicking the pile of plastic tests out of the way, I got down on my knees next to Claire and pulled her into my arms. She sobbed and mumbled random facts about sperm and I reminded myself to tell her at a later point to stay the fuck away from the library reference books. No good can come from those things.

I reached down with one hand and picked up a test from the pile and sure enough, a big, fat pink plus sign was right smack in the middle of it. My heart dropped to my toes and I felt like crying myself all of a sudden.

"Maybe the tests are wrong. They could be wrong, right? Women get false positives all the time. I saw it on Oprah," Claire rambled as she snot all over the shoulder of my shirt. "This one woman thought she was pregnant and when it came time to deliver, she found out it was a giant tumor. Maybe I have a tumor? A tumor masking itself as a baby. Both of them could suck the life right out of me and make me want to die, but I think I'd rather have a tumor. You can remove a tumor and never have to see it again. You can't do that with a baby, right?"

I tossed the pregnancy test down onto the pile of others and rested my cheek on top of her head. "I hate to break it to you, but I'm pretty sure it's not a tumor. I don't think you'd get twenty-seven positive pregnancy tests out of a tumor."

"Thirty-two," Claire mumbled. "I took five at the grocery store while I drank the milk."

We sat on the floor of our dingy bathroom and I let her cry it out for a few minutes before I spoke again.

"Are you going to tell me who the rat bastard is so I can chop off his balls?"

That just started a whole new round of wailing and crying from Claire and I did my best to calm her down, but nothing worked.

"I'm a slut! I'm a dirty, dirty slut! I had a one-night stand at a frat party and I didn't even get his name! I'm the girl parents warn their daughters about. They're going to put my face on a billboard telling teenage girls what NOT to do. MY LIFE IS OVER!"

I turned to face Claire and grabbed her shoulders, forcing her to look at me. "Stop it, right now. No one talks about my best friend like that, got it? I shouldn't have pushed you so much to lose your virginity to the first guy who came along. It's that douchebag's fault for not using a fucking condom! We are going to get through this, Claire. You're going to dry your eyes and stop the girly crying shit. You're stronger than this! You are a total badass and I am not about to let you wallow in misery. We're going to get up, get out of this bathroom and go hunt this motherfucker down."

She nodded her head during my speech, so hopefully

I was doing *something* right. I didn't even bring up adoption or abortion because even though Claire never ever wanted to have kids, she was definitely pro-life and one of those women who owned up to her mistakes and took whatever consequences came her way, including having a baby.

Jesus Christ, my best friend was going to have a baby.

"First thing we're going to do is feed you. Have you even eaten anything today?" I asked as I got up from the floor and pulled her up right along with me.

"Are we counting the milk, because I'm pretty sure an entire gallon should be considered its own food group."

I shook my head at her and she sighed.

"Well, I had seven sticks of string cheese and an entire loaf of bread before I went to the store to buy the tests," she replied. "Also, we're out of bread. And string cheese."

I wrapped my arm around her shoulder and led her out of the bathroom. "I'm going to call Jim and see if he can do some detective work to find out who this guy is. If anything, we'll just go back to the frat house during the day when there's a chance of them being sober and see if they know who he is."

"Just promise me you won't kick his ass," Claire begged.

"Why the hell shouldn't I kick his ass? He knocked you up and never even told you his name," I argued.

"We were drunk! It's not like I told him my name

either," she fired back. "He was nice, Liz, really nice. I was the idiot who snuck out of the bedroom the next morning and did the walk of shame out of the house."

I really couldn't argue with her at that point. When I finally made it home after spending the day with Jim the day after the party, I was completely ecstatic that she'd finally done the deed. I almost shed a few tears when she told me how she hit it and quit it and never looked back. My girl was finally all grown up and taking a page out of my book. Minus the whole getting knocked up at a frat party thing.

"Fine, so he was a nice guy. I still think he needs his ass kicked on principle alone. For your sake, we'll do this nice and civilized. We'll ask around and we'll find him. I mean, how hard can it be? Ohio University isn't that big. We're bound to find someone who knows who this guy is."

Claire took a few deep breaths and wiped the remaining tears from her face. She put her chin up and had a look of determination on her face. "You're right. How hard *can* it be?"

I grabbed Claire's purse from the desk next to our bunks and handed it to her, throwing my own over my shoulder as we headed for the door to pound pavement and find her baby daddy.

"No matter what happens, I'm going to be here for you, okay? I know it really sucks right now, but you're not alone. That baby is going to be the coolest kid in the entire fucking world because he has you for a mom and me for an aunt."

Claire smiled at me as I held the door open for her. "We should probably try cutting back on our swearing before this thing gets here. I don't think its first words should be 'fuck' or 'kiss my ass'."

I shrugged as I locked the door behind us and we headed downstairs. "Could you imagine having a kid who repeated everything we say? Kid would be a Goddamn genius, I'm telling you."

Chapter 8

Rack of Ribs

"YOU CAN'T IGNORE her forever."

I look up from a pile of paperwork at my desk and scowl when I see Jim standing in the doorway of my office at Seduction and Snacks. Now that Gavin and Charlotte both worked at headquarters, Claire and I had been able to spend more time lately in our flagship store, our baby and where we loved to be.

"I have no idea what you're talking about," I tell him.

I look away from him and back down at my paperwork so he can't see my eyes and know I'm lying. It's stupid. I know it's stupid. He knows I'm lying, I know I'm lying, EVERYONE knows I'm lying.

Claire has been home from the hospital for three days and I haven't gone to see her. I'm ashamed of myself but what the fuck am I supposed to do? I'm scared to death. I have no control of this situation and it makes me want to scream.

"I talked to Carter last night. He said she's doing really good and sleeping a lot," I tell him.

"Hon, you have to go see her. She *needs* you," Jim reminds me.

I slam my pen down on top of the desk and stare at him. "She doesn't need me! She needs a fucking cure for what's happened to her and I can't give that to her. For the first time in our friendship I can't do anything to help her and it's fucking killing me!"

I swallow back the tears, refusing to cry. I know once I start, I'll never be able to stop. I've been working like a maniac since Claire got out of surgery and the doctor told us she was stable and the surgery went well. I didn't know what else to do. After Carter's breakdown in their kitchen and the shaved cat incident, I drove right to Seduction and Snacks and buried myself in work. Working takes my mind off of things I can't control. Work is the only thing keeping me sane right now. Who knew that organizing orders of butt plugs and anal beads would actually keep my insanity at bay?

"She doesn't need you to fix her, Liz. She just needs you to be there for her," Jim tells me softly as he walks across the room and squats down next to me.

He grabs onto the seat of my chair and spins me so that I'm facing him.

"It's too hard," I whisper.

Jim rests his hands on my thighs and rubs his thumbs comfortingly over my skin. "I know it is, babe. You guys have been through a lot together but this is the worst. Through thick and thin, isn't that what best friends are all about? What would Claire do if the situation were reversed? I'm guessing she'd be all up your ass and pissing you off so much that you forgot all about what was happening. That's all she needs from you right now. She just needs to know that you're there and you care."

Of course I care. It's absurd for anyone to think otherwise. She's my person, my other half. I care so much that it's killing me right now not to be there for her, but I don't know what to say and I don't know what to do. That whole saying about actions speaking louder than words runs through my mind and just like that, I know exactly what to do. It will most likely piss Claire off, but maybe it will take her mind off of things and in my own way, I can show her that I'm sorry for flaking on her the last few days.

I give my husband a quick kiss and grab my phone, calling Jenny and getting her on board with my plan.

"Do you know how hard it was to get an appointment at the last minute?" Jenny complains as we walk up the sidewalk to Claire and Carter's front porch.

When I called her earlier, she was about two hours away meeting with a new marketing company and said she wouldn't be able to make it back in time to join me for my own appointment. I wouldn't let myself get discouraged though and told her to just do it on her own and then we'd meet up later tonight at Claire's house.

"Quit your bitching, Claire is going to love this," I tell her as I knock a couple of times on the door to announce our presence before walking inside.

"Are you sure she's going to like this? It makes absolutely no sense," Jenny complains.

I have no idea what she's talking about and I don't have time to argue with her because as soon as we get in the house, I see Claire sitting on the couch under a pile of blankets.

She looks pale and tired and I panic for a minute. I shouldn't want to run away from my best friend, but I do. I want to turn around and run out the door and pretend like this isn't happening. I want to close my eyes and walk back into the house and imagine that it's three months ago when I walked through the door to celebrate her birthday and she was already halfway to being trashed, her face flushed and her smile bright as she called me a bag of dicks and thrust a beer in my hand.

"Claire, you look like shit," Jenny tells her.

I smack Jenny's arm as Claire laughs.

"I feel like shit too," Claire informs us with a low, raspy voice.

Carter walks into the living room from the kitchen with a glass of ice water and sets it down on the coffee table in front of her. I watch him slide his arms behind her and help her sit up and I want to scream. She's the strongest person I've ever met and she needs help sitting up on the couch. I should have been the one to race over there and help her. I should have instinctively known she needed help but I didn't. Or maybe I did but I'm just too fucking scared to get close to her.

"We have a surprise for you!" Jenny announces as Carter fusses over Claire's blankets and she smacks his hands away.

Carter starts to walk away but immediately stops in his tracks when Jenny pulls her shirt all the way up until her tits pop out.

"Is that the surprise, because I like it," Carter says with a nod.

"Oh, for God's sakes," I mutter, grabbing onto the hem of my shirt and tugging it up just enough to show off the skin over my ribs.

Claire stares back and forth between Jenny and I, a look of confusion on her face.

"One of these things is not like the other," Claire sing-songs.

I lean forward to get a look at Jenny's side, trying to

avoid her tits hanging out for the world to see.

"What in the fuck is that?" I shout, pointing to whatever the hell it is.

Jenny looks down at herself and then back at me. "It's what you told me to do! I'll admit, it sounded a little weird when you told me on the phone, but I kind of like it and it totally makes sense."

Carter cocks his head to the side and squints. "I believe what we're looking at is a rack of ribs tattoo. Awesome!"

I turn to face her, pointing to my own tattoo. "Pink ribbon on our ribs, Jenny! PINK RIBBON ON OUR RIBS! How in the hell does a rack of ribs make any kind of sense right now?"

Jenny stares at me in confusion for a few minutes and then the light goes on. "Ohhhhhhh, yeah. I guess that makes sense. But, I mean, it's a rack. Get it? Save your rack? I really think mine is better."

Jesus Christ, when I called Jenny and told her we should get matching tattoos of a pink ribbon in support of Claire, I should have known she'd get it all wrong. I never should have let her do it on her own.

"Well, the sentiment was nice," Claire tells us with a shrug, trying to hide her laugh.

"Dammit, now I'm hungry for ribs," Carter complains.

Jenny finally pulls her shirt down and walks over to the couch, flopping down next to Claire. "Drew has been driving me insane since I got the tattoo earlier. He keeps wanting to lick it because he's convinced it will taste like barbeque."

Carter scrunches up his face in disgust. "And now I'll never be hungry for ribs ever again. Thank you for that."

Carter leaves us alone, most likely to go throw up somewhere and an awkward silence fills the room when he's gone.

Thankfully, Jenny doesn't know how to shut up for more than two seconds so she starts rattling on and on about barbeque sauce in places one should NEVER put barbeque sauce and I tune her out.

Claire stares right at me like she's waiting for me to say something. I know I should apologize for not coming over sooner, but I can't make the words come out. Is there a book called *How to Talk to Your Best Friend When She Has Breast Cancer For Dummies?* I might need that. I've always been there for her when she needed me. I've always known the right things to say, why should now be any different? Maybe because all the times in the past weren't life or death situations. To quote *The Breakfast Club*, when Claire messed with the bull, I shoved my horns up someone's ass to make them pay. Okay, I'm paraphrasing there, but whatever.

If Claire had a problem, I fixed it. End of story. Why in the fuck can't I fix this? Why can't we just go back to when things were crazy and fun and I could make everything better for her?

Chapter 9

Meat Curtains

Twenty-five years ago...

"THIS IS FUCKING BULLSHIT! If you don't have drugs then get the fuck out of my room!" Claire screamed at the poor nurse who came in to take her vitals.

The nurse took one look at Claire, told her she'd come back later and ran from the room.

"Oh, that was really nice. Great attitude, Miss Exorcist. Will there be green vomit spewing from your mouth for your next trick?" I asked as I handed her a cup of ice chips.

She snatched the cup out of my hand and snarled at me. "Eat. A bag. Of Dicks."

"Classy. I hope those are your son's first words," I

told her as I pulled a chair up to the edge of the bed and sat down.

"Where the hell is Jim? He left like three hours ago to get me a grape Popsicle. I WANT MY FUCKING GRAPE POPSICLE!" Claire screamed.

"He left five minutes ago, cranky ass," I reminded her.

Claire had been in labor for exactly one hour. ONE HOUR and she was already losing her shit. I feared for anyone within a mile radius of this woman when she actually had to start pushing that thing out of her.

"Come on, it can't hurt *that* bad," I joked, dodging out of the way when her hand flew up to smack me. "I'm kidding! Jesus, you know I'm kidding. Lighten up, dude. After today, you'll finally be able to see your feet. And just think of all the booze you can drink in the middle of the night when you can't sleep because he's screaming his fool head off."

Claire started to curse at me, but thankfully another contraction ripped through her and she had to concentrate on breathing instead of kicking my ass.

I grabbed onto her hand and let her squeeze the life out of it, watching the contraction monitor next to her bed and letting her know when it was almost over.

"You're doing good, keep breathing, just a few more seconds."

When it passed, she let out a huge sigh and slumped back against her pillows.

She turned her head and stared at me, tears filling her eyes. "I'm so scared, Liz."

I knew immediately she wasn't talking about the whole pushing a human out of her body-thing. While that thought was scary and more than a little bit gross, I knew she was thinking about what happened *after* he was here. She was a strong woman who could handle a few hours of pain, but I could tell just by looking at her that she was second-guessing her ability to be a mom.

"You're going to be fine. He's going to come out and he's going to be perfect and you're going to be FINE. It's going to suck for a while and you're going to miss out on a lot of sleep and you'll probably never take another uninterrupted shower or piss again, but it's going to be okay, I promise you. You are amazing and you're strong and you're going to get through this. You've got me and Jim and your father and we're going to be there every step of the way. No matter what you're worrying about right now, just remember that you aren't alone. You will *never* be alone. I've got you, babe."

Another contraction hit and I stood up, brushing her hair off of her face and helping her count through the pain. I felt so helpless that I couldn't make the pain go away, but it didn't matter. For the first time in our lives, this was something she had to do on her own. All I could do was be there for her and help her any way I could. I decided that humor was always the best medicine. I couldn't take the pain from her, but I could make her laugh.

"So, have you thought about how horrific your vagina is going to look after you push that little guy out? Like meat curtains flapping in the breeze every time you walk. Man, your poor vagina."

Claire attempted to call me an asshole, but she couldn't get the words out. She started laughing instead. "Oh, my God! It's going to look like a wilted, roast beef sandwich."

"Jesus, I'm never going to be able to eat at Arby's again. Thank you for THAT visual," I told her with a shudder. "On the bright side, it could be a great pick-up line. 'Hey, there hot stuff. Do you like beef? I've got some in my pants just for you.'"

Claire rested her hands on her huge stomach as she continued laughing. "Vagina, the other white meat."

"Beefy vagina: it's what's for dinner!" I shouted.

The doctor chose that moment to walk in the room. He looked at both of us, laughing so hard we were crying and I shrugged my shoulders. "Just giving her a little encouragement, Doctor. Would you like to place your vagina bet? I've got ten to one odds right now that her vagina will resemble ground zero of a bomb blast. What say you?"

The doctor ignored us, pulling the privacy curtain around the bed to block the doorway. "I'm just going to check on you and see how things are progressing. How are the contractions?"

"They hurt like a motherfucker," Claire told him honestly.

"Good, good. That means things are moving along."

I quickly reached over and grabbed onto Claire's legs when I saw a look of murder in her eyes. She was about one second away from kicking the good doctor in the face.

Once he got the blanket pushed up over her knees, he snapped on a pair of rubber gloves and went to town between my friend's legs.

"Don't look. Whatever you do, you are NOT allowed to look down there," Claire threatened.

She winced at whatever the doctor was doing and I winced right back in sympathy. "No need for *that* warning. I wasn't about to stick my head down there to get a look at the crime scene you've got going on between your legs."

The curtain suddenly slid open. "Who wants a grape Popsicle?!"

Claire and I both looked up at Jim and watched the smile on his face fall.

"Oh, no," he muttered as the Popsicle dropped out of his hand and hit the floor.

"OH, MY GOD! GET OUT! STOP LOOKING!" Claire and I both shouted at the same time.

My poor fiancé didn't budge.

"Monster. Help. Popsicle scary," he mumbled.

Claire tried to close her legs but the doctor was knee deep in vagina and there was nothing she could do.

"GET OUT RIGHT NOW!" we both screamed in unison again.

His eyes were glazed over at this point and I was thanking God we were in a hospital because I was pretty sure he was going to pass out any minute now.

"I like Popsicles. And puppies. Just think about puppies," he muttered to himself.

When I realized that my poor man was in a pregnant woman vagina daze-slash-nightmare, I took action. I hustled around to the end of the bed and stood in front of him, blocking his view.

"Breathe, Jim. BREATHE!" I reminded him.

He took a huge breath and finally blinked. "I'm just gonna leave."

I nodded at him and turned him around, pushing him back towards the door. "That's a great idea, honey. How about you just go back into the waiting room with Claire's dad and never, ever step foot in this room again, okay?"

"Never step foot in this room again?" he questioned as I walked him to the door.

"That's right, never step foot in this room again. Good boy."

I patted him on the back and shoved him into the hallway, closing the door to the room behind me before going back to Claire's bedside.

"Your future husband saw my vagina," Claire stated.

"Better him than me."

The doctor stood up, pulling his gloves off and tossing them into the trash next to the bed. "Well, you haven't dilated at all, but it's still early. We're going to put a fetal heart monitor on the baby just to make sure he's handling the contractions okay and I'm going to have one of the nurses give you some Pitocin to try and move things along. I'll come back to check on you in a little while."

A few hours later, long after the Pitocin and Claire threatening to kill everyone who came near her, the doctor decided it was time for an emergency C-section. Claire was scared to death. I was scared to death. Everything started happening so fast at that point. Doctors and nurses were running around, making calls and before we knew it, Claire was being wheeled out of her room and down the hall to the operating room.

I jogged next to her bed and never let go of her hand the entire way. I knew she was freaking out and I didn't know what the hell to do other than make sure she understood that I'd always be here for her.

"You're not going to leave, right?" Claire asked when we got into the brightly lit OR and they transferred her to another bed.

I squeezed her hand tighter as one of the nurses handed me a pair of scrubs and a hospital mask. "I'm *never* going to leave you. I'm going to be here the entire time.

It's just you and me, Claire, you and me."

She nodded her head as the nurses started putting up sheets around her body so we couldn't see what was going on below her chest.

"You and me," she agreed.

"You can do this. You've totally got this. It's going to be over soon and Gavin is going to be here and he's going to be healthy and perfect and we're going to start teaching him how to swear before he shits his pants for the first time."

Claire laughed and I quickly threw on the scrubs over my clothes and took my seat next to Claire's bed.

Right at that moment, I knew that I would do anything for my best friend. I would hold her hand when she was in pain, scream at my catatonic fiancé when he saw her vagina and sit by her side when she became a mom. There was nothing I wouldn't do for her and I knew that's how it would always be.

Chapter 10

It's All About You

"I HAVE LAURIE running things at the bakery for the next six weeks and you don't have any weddings or big events coming up, so I think she can handle it. Jenny is going to take over ordering baking supplies and she's going to help Laurie and your two part-time girls do all the baking," I explain, going down the list of items I put in my notepad app on my phone. "If any big orders come in, we can always get some more help in, but I think we'll be fine. We'll have to put the Friday Freebie cupcake sale on hold for the time being, but I don't think too many people will mind."

Claire grabs my cell phone out of my hand and I finally look up at her. I wish I hadn't. I wish I still had my phone in my hand to give me something else to stare at, something to keep myself occupied so I don't have to see what is happening to her. I'm a shitty friend and an even shittier person because I can't bear to look at my best friend and see what the chemo has done to her hair. Every time she runs her fingers through her hair or brushes up against the back of the couch, more strands come out, but she just shrugs her shoulders like it's no big deal. One round of chemo almost three weeks ago and she's already losing her hair. She still has five more rounds to go and I'm scared to death she's just going to keep fading away until there's nothing left of her.

"I've hired some extra help at my store so I'll be able to pop over to your side as much as I want," I continue. "We were supposed to do that interview with the local television station next week, but I called them and told them to postpone it. I'll keep a file with all your invoices and bring them over when you need to sign something so you won't need to—"

"Will you shut up already?" Claire interrupts. "Stop talking about work when we both know there's something a little more important we need to discuss."

I shake my head and grab my phone back from her. "No, it's fine. We don't need to talk about it. You don't need to think about it. We can just talk about fun things like work and how Jenny has decided to start breeding ferrets now that the kids are in college and she's bored."

"As disturbing as that is, I don't want to talk about

the damn ferrets," Claire tells me. "Wait, she was serious about breeding ferrets?"

I nod my head. "You don't even want to know where she got that idea. There's something called Fur Fest that she and Drew want to attend and she thinks she needs to breed something exotic and furry in order to fit in. I Googled Fur Fest. I can never get back those five minutes. So anyway, things are running smoothly at the shop and I don't foresee any issues with—"

Claire reaches over and presses her hand over my mouth.

"Stop. Talking. About. Work. I had a double mastectomy four weeks ago and a round of chemo that is kicking my ass and I can count on one hand how many times I've seen you during all of this. I get it; it's scary. What I don't get is why you won't even fucking *talk* about it with me."

I move my face away from her hand and get up from the couch to pace around the room. I can't sit still for this. I need to keep moving or I'm going to completely break down and that's not what she needs right now.

"You need to accept the fact that this is happening. It's real. You can't keep pretending like everything is okay," she tells me softly.

I stop pacing and make myself look in her general direction. It hurts too much to look right at her—my best friend, so small and tired and run down, sitting on the couch with blankets tucked around her as her beautiful brown hair is quickly disappearing. "I'm trying, Claire. I don't want to talk about it all the time and keep reminding you about what's happening."

Claire throws her hands up in the air in irritation. "You don't think I'm reminded of this fucking disease every damn time I take a breath or look in the mirror? Every time I open my eyes, every time I MOVE it's there, trying to bring me down. It's all I fucking think about and you pretending like it's not real is what's really killing me."

Her words cut right through me and I can't help but gasp.

"Jesus Christ, you just compared me to…"

"CANCER! Fucking say it, Liz. I compared you to cancer. I have cancer. You can't even fucking say it!" Claire screams.

"NO! I can't fucking say it because you're right! I don't want it to be real. I don't want this to be happening right now. I don't want you to be sick. I can't stand the fact that there is absolutely NOTHING I can do to make this better!" I shout back.

She flings the blankets off of her and gets up from the couch, stalking over to me.

"You still don't get it! This isn't about YOU! You can't fix it, you can't make it better, you don't know what to say, you don't know what to do. YOU, YOU, YOU! This is happening to ME, Goddammit, and I just need my fucking friend! Why can't you just be my friend? This is out of everyone's control, especially yours. If you can't deal with that then you need to get the fuck out of my house."

We stand toe-to-toe, both of us wearing equal looks of anger. As much as I don't have the right to be mad at her, I can't help it. This was never supposed to happen. Our friendship was solid and I thought nothing could ever break it. She's pissed at me for not being a good friend and I'm pissed at her for not understanding that I don't know HOW to be a good friend if I'm not the one making things better. She knows I'm a control freak, how can she possibly expect me to not feel helpless about this?

"I'm sorry I'm not perfect!" I fire back. "My friend gets sick and I don't know what the fuck to do, so sue me! I'm trying here and you're not making it any easier. You want to talk, talk, talk about this horrible thing that's happening and I can't do that. I can't just act like it's the most natural thing in the world to talk about my best friend having breast cancer! I'm not a sappy, talk about my feelings kind of person and you should damn well know that by now. I got a fucking tattoo to show you I cared, I'm taking care of your shop so you can rest and I'm trying to take your mind off of things because I don't know what else to do!"

Claire takes a step back and crosses her arms across her chest. "I never asked you to get a tattoo, nor did I ask you for help with the shop. All I needed was my best friend to tell me everything will be okay and you can't even do that. I know it's horseshit. I know we don't know if everything will be okay, but I need YOU to believe that. How the hell am I supposed to believe it if you don't? You can't even LOOK at me!"

I realize I've been staring at a button on her shirt the entire time she spoke and quickly look up to meet her eyes. I don't know what she sees on my face but it's enough for her to shake her head at me.

"Just get out," she tells me sadly.

I'm so pissed that she's ordering me out of the house I don't even think about the fact that this is the first real fight we've ever had in thirty years of friendship and I'm not sure if we'll ever be able to recover from it.

"Fine! I'm out of here!" I scream back.

I walk away from my best friend and let the front door slam behind me. I get to my car and let the anger flow through me as I pull out of the driveway and head home. My anger festers and builds until I get inside my house, throw my purse across the kitchen and head to my bedroom. It all disappears as soon as I flop down on my bed and realize what just happened. I curl my legs up to my chest and, for the first time since Claire told us what was going on, I let myself cry. I cry so hard and for so long that I can't breathe. I keep right on sobbing when I feel the bed dip behind me and Jim curls up against me, wrapping his arms around me and holding me close. He doesn't say a word, he just lets me cry.

I can't believe I screamed at my best friend. She's got cancer, she's sick and she's scared and I stood in her living room and yelled at her. What kind of person does that? I should have just taken what she threw at me. She deserves to scream and yell and let it all out. She's right, it's not all about me. It was never about me, it was always about her. This is *her* battle and *her* illness and as much as I want to, I can't fight it for her. I was supposed to be the one who always understood her, but at the first sign of trouble, I forgot everything about being a good friend and what she would need from me. I didn't talk about what was going on with her because it was too hard for me, but it shouldn't have mattered. What she's going through is a thousand times worse than what I'm going through. I am a selfish person and I let Claire down.

I was so scared of losing my best friend to this disease that I never stopped to think that I might just loser her because of my own pig-headedness instead. She's been there through all of my good times and I let her down during one of her worst times. I just want to go back to the good times. It was so much easier then.

Chapter 11

Balloon Fucker

Twenty-two years ago, in a balloon galaxy far, far away...

JIM AND I planned getting pregnant, so it wasn't much of a surprise when the stick turned pink. It wasn't a huge secret because we'd been talking about it and trying our hardest to make it happen for months, but I still wanted to do something special to break the news to him. I hate surprises and being the center of attention, but Jim loves it so I really wanted to plan something special to tell him. I would have been perfectly fine just blurting it out over dinner and being done with it, but Jim is a romantic and he wouldn't be too pleased with that.

I asked Jim to meet me at Seduction and Snacks one night under the guise of helping me with inventory. When he walked in, his face took on a look of confusion when he saw the entire place filled with balloons. Piles of green, purple, red, blue and orange balloons littered the floor and every available surface of the shop and hundreds more filled with helium covered every inch of the ceiling. I could have gone with pink and blue, but I didn't want to make it too obvious.

Jim kicked balloons out of the way, making a path as he walked towards me. He opened his mouth to speak, but was immediately interrupted by Drew, who came running in from Claire's side of the store.

"This is the best day EVER!" Drew shouted, holding the largest balloon I had ever seen in his hands.

Jim looked at me questioningly.

"Sorry, this was kind of his idea, so I told him he could help," I explained.

I watched as Drew raced back and forth among the balloons like a two-year old on crack. "Tell him the best part! TELL HIM THE BEST PART!"

I grabbed my husband's hands and squeezed them. "I have a surprise for you. Drew thought it should be something fun. So, if you want to know what your surprise is, you'll need to pop the balloons until you find the one it's hidden in."

I managed to slide the positive pregnancy test into one of the balloons before we blew it up and it was somewhere in this room, although I'd lost track of it ever since Drew came barreling in here.

"OH, MY GOD! POP THEM! POP THEM!" Drew shouted as he swatted at balloons that floated up and down from the ceiling.

Before I could question how much caffeine Drew had ingested to make him so excitable, Claire, Carter and Jenny stepped in from Claire's side of the store and made their way over to the counter where the cash register was.

"Don't mind us," Claire announced. "We're just here to huff some helium."

Jenny immediately grabbed a ribbon attached to a balloon on the ceiling, yanked it towards her and went to work untying it while Drew finally stopped running to stand in front of Jim. He held the giant balloon he'd been racing around with out to him. "Please, pop this one first."

Jim laughed before taking the balloon from Drew's hand.

"Mmmmmm yeah, pop that balloon," Drew moaned as Jim started squeezing it.

Jim paused and looked up at him. "Why are you moaning?"

Drew didn't answer. His eyes glazed over as Jim squeezed harder and when the balloon popped, I swear to God his legs almost gave out and his eyes rolled to the back of his head.

Since Jim didn't find the pregnancy test in that

balloon, he went to work walking around the store, stomping on balloons as he went. I couldn't help but notice that Drew was following close behind Jim. Every time he popped another balloon, Drew's voice got deeper and more sexual as he cheered him on and it really started to creep me the fuck out. I couldn't even complain to my friends, though, because they were all sucking helium and cracking each other up.

"We represent, the Lollypop Guild, the Lollypop Guild, the Lollypop Guild!" Carter sang in a squeaky, high-pitched voice. Everyone laughed while Drew got right up by my ear.

"Tell Jim he should pop that red one next. It's so round and full and when it pops it's going to make this great noise and the smell of rubber will fill the air…" he trailed off and his entire body shuddered.

"What in the actual fuck is happening with you right now?"

Drew ignored me, bending down to grab a red balloon. He rubbed it over his chest and sighed before handing it to Jim.

"I am not touching that thing now that you fondled it," Jim told him.

His eyes widened. "Can I pop it? Please, please, please, can I, can I, can I?!"

"You can pop every fucking balloon in here if it means you'll stop looking like you want to have sex with the damn things," Jim told him in disgust as Drew hummed while he squeezed the balloon.

"Drew is a Looner," Jenny yelled over to me in a helium-filled voice.

"What the hell is a Looner?" Claire asked in the same munchkin-like, helium tone.

"A Looner is a very complex individual who revels in the popping of balloons," Carter informed us, sounding like a cast-off from Wizard of Oz.

When everyone looked at him funny, he just shrugged. "I Googled it."

"Ha! Now I know why Drew wanted to fill this place with balloons," Claire announced before taking another hit of helium. "Drew is a balloon fucker!"

Now, one would think that hearing the words "balloon fucker" coming from the mouth of my best friend who sounded like she was from Munchkin Land would have been hilarious. However, Drew was now on all fours down by my feet, dry humping a balloon.

"OH, MY GOD! WHAT ARE YOU DOING?!" I screamed at him.

"I'm only doing what comes naturally! My balloon fetish is a form of sexual imprinting! YOU CAN'T STOP ME FROM SEXUALLY IMPRINTING ON THIS GREEN BALLOON!" Drew shouted as he thrust roughly against the balloon until it popped.

As soon as it exploded, I heard the *click-click-click* of a plastic pregnancy test bouncing across the floor.

"WOOOHOOO! You found the balloon with the

surprise in it! Pick it up and show it to Jim!" Carter squeaked with his fists pumping in the air.

"If you think I am going to touch something that Drew just humped out of a balloon, you are sadly mistaken," I told him.

"Whew, that was exhausting. I think I need a nap," Drew announced, grabbing onto an orange balloon and sticking it under his head like a pillow.

Jim ran across the room, shoving balloons aside until he found the test on the floor a few feet away. He picked it up, stared at it in awe for a few minutes before walking back to me.

"Liz, are you serious?! Are you—"

"WE WELCOME YOU TO MUNCHKIN LAND!" Jenny sang loudly, dissolving in a fit of giggles as she quickly grabbed another balloon from the ceiling while Claire and Carter took a big huff of the balloons in each of their hands.

I sighed, turning back to Jim to finally tell him out loud what he already knew was true. "I love you. We're going to have a—"

"Tra la la la la la la la la la la la!" Carter and Claire squeaked at the top of their tinny voices.

"When you guys are finished, can I spend some time alone here in the shop?" Drew suddenly questioned.

"Ashtray! You little bitch ass motherfucker! Come over here and give your grandma a hug!" Carter shouted in his helium voice, because quoting *Don't Be a Menace* while huffing helium is always a fine idea.

"Bitch ass motherfucker!" Jenny repeated.

"I'VE HAD IT WITH THESE MOTHERFUCKING SNAKES ON THIS MOTHERFUCKING PLANE!" Claire shouted.

Jesus Christ, it sounded like Munchkins gone wild in this place.

"How about we just cut to the chase?" I asked Jim, wrapping my arms around his shoulders. "We're going to have a baby. As soon as he or she is born, we are getting as far away from these idiots as possible."

Jim wrapped his arms around me and we stared at our friends who were now trading Samuel L. Jackson quotes back and forth in between sucking on the balloons.

"Awwww, come on, our friends are fun. Just think about how interesting your baby shower will be. We can have Drew do balloon animals for the kids," Jim laughed.

"Except that would turn into Drew actually DOING balloon animals," I reminded him.

"Well, one thing's for certain—our life will never be boring with these people in it," Jim told me.

As Carter wrapped his arms around Claire and whispered high-pitched sexual innuendos in her ear, Jenny ran over to Drew and flopped down on the floor next to him and they both started rubbing balloons all over themselves.

"You're right, life will never be boring with any of them," I agreed.

Chapter 12

Say Cheese!

MY FAMILY AND I are pretty lucky in that we've never had to deal with losing someone close to us. My kids still have all four grandparents and our extended family of aunts, uncles and cousins are alive and kicking. It's probably hard to believe, but we've only attended one funeral. Ever. It was for one of our neighbors a few years ago. She was a nasty old woman who screamed at my kids if they so much as *looked* at her yard when they walked by and she had a habit of stealing people's Christmas decorations if she thought they were too gaudy. We only went to the funeral for her husband, who was the exact opposite of the old bat. Also, we were hoping our blinking "Santa Stops Here" sign might be perched in front of the casket so we could take it back. I loved that cute little sign.

Looking back on it now, I'm kind of glad that was our one and only experience with a funeral because we did not behave well. We tried, we really did, but it was no use.

Six years ago, when a funeral home suddenly became the best place on earth...

"I'VE GOT A camera on my cell phone!"

My daughter, Charlotte, and I looked up at the little boy standing next to my chair. He was around seven years old and he proudly held an old school flip phone in his hand.

I glanced around at the other mourners who filled the room in row after row of folding chairs, but no one seemed to be looking for their lost child.

"That's a great phone," I whispered to the boy. "You should probably go take some pictures or something."

Jim leaned forward in his seat on the other side of Charlotte and gave me a questioning look. I just shrugged. I didn't know who the hell this kid was, but I was pretty sure he needed to leave me alone. I had three teenage daughters who were lucky I even liked them, let alone loved them. I didn't do well with other people's children.

"My name is Luke. I like chocolate!" the kid announced.

"I can see that. You've got it smeared all over your

damn face," I replied, scrunching up my nose in disgust as he leaned his dirty face closer to me.

"You said a bad word!" he whispered.

"I'm going to keep on saying bad words if you don't go away."

Charlotte snorted and Jim just shook his head.

"That's my grandma up there," Luke said, pointing to the open casket at the front of the room. "She's dead."

This just made Charlotte laugh harder for some reason. She covered her mouth with her hand to stifle the noise and I elbowed her to shut up. I'm pretty sure this room of sad people wouldn't be too happy to hear her laughing like a hyena.

"Okay, dude, run along now. Go take some pictures."

I was starting to get a little uncomfortable with this kid. He was a regular Chatty Cathy and this was supposed to be a quiet time of reflection for the deceased or some shit before the priest came in and said a few words.

I was so busy trying to shush Charlotte that I didn't notice that the stupid kid decided to listen to me. He ran along, and he definitely took some pictures. You know how those old flip phones would make noises when you took a picture like the clicking of a camera or something else equally annoying? Well, in the middle of "quiet time," when half the room was crying softly and the other half was deep in prayer or whatever, at the front of the room, right in front of the casket was our little buddy Luke. He had his flip phone open, pointed directly at the dead body of Mrs. Lyons. I'm pretty sure we were the only people in the room who saw what he was about to do, but that all changed as soon as he hit the "take picture" button. In the quiet, somber room filled with death and sadness, the mechanical, overly cheerful voice of the flip phone said "SAY CHEEEEEEEESE!" followed by the *click* of the shutter releasing.

"Jesus Christ, did he just take a picture of his dead grandma?" Jim whispered.

Charlotte was laughing so hard at this point she started choking. I couldn't believe what the fuck had just happened and for some reason, it became the funniest shit in the entire world. I clamped my hand over my mouth to keep the giggles contained, but that didn't stop my shoulders from shaking as Charlotte and I huddled together, both of us whispering, "Say cheese!" in between our snorts of laughter.

Luke's mother finally got her head out of her ass and came running down the center aisle, snatching the phone out of his hand as she gave us a dirty look.

"We did NOT put him up to that!" I whispered as she made her way down the aisle past us, dragging Luke behind her.

Charlotte let out a cough/snort/laugh that was so loud, the entire room was now looking at us. Our very first funeral and we were going to get kicked out of it. Everything just became funny at that point and it didn't help that Charlotte kept whispering "say cheese" and "I wonder if I could get a five by seven of that shot?" We decided to make things easy on everyone and excused ourselves from the funeral before they asked us to leave. Really, I think that little bastard Luke should have been the one to get kicked out. He started it.

I FIND MYSELF thinking about that funeral and how my children have no idea how to deal with death and sadness or something awful happening to someone close to them. Charlotte sits across from me at the kitchen table looking miserable and I'm at a loss on how to help my child. How can I help her when I don't even know how to help myself? She's no longer a fifteen year old at the funeral of the mean neighbor lady. Her fiancé's mother, the woman she herself thinks of as an aunt, is sick and it's scary and that little asshole Luke isn't here to diffuse the situation with inappropriate pictures of his dead grandmother. My daughter needs my help and I need to find a way to give it to her.

"What should I do, mom? Gavin is trying to act all strong and he keeps telling me he's fine, but I know he's not. I know he's freaking out and I don't know what to do," Charlotte tells me as tears fill her eyes.

"Honey, all you can do is let him know that you're

there for him. He's going to continue being strong and not showing any emotion in front of Claire because he doesn't want his mom to see how much he's hurting," I explain. "He's a guy. Guys don't want anyone to know they're scared. Look at his father. Carter has been rearranging their house and putting everything in alphabetical order. That's his way of coping."

Charlotte lets out a sigh and I move my chair to her side of the table, wrapping my arms around her.

"He's my best friend, mom. I don't want him to be scared. I just want to make everything better for him, but I can't. I hate feeling so helpless."

I always thought my oldest daughter and I were so different. She was always the bubbly, happy girl who made friends easily and looked at life with rose-colored glasses. Right now, I realize we're more alike than I ever knew.

"All of this is out of everyone's control and it sucks. Maybe he just needs you to tell him how you're feeling and that he's not alone. Be honest with him. Be there for him. That's all you really *can* do right now."

Guilt overwhelms me as I hold my daughter and let her cry. It's easy for me to give her this great advice. Why isn't it easy for me to follow it myself?

"I don't want Aunt Claire to die," Charlotte whispers.

My throat tightens and I squeeze my eyes closed to keep the tears from falling.

"Do you remember the first time I got my period,

you guys both showed me how to put a panty-liner in my underwear?" Charlotte suddenly asks with a laugh.

We both sniffle through our laughter, remembering that day.

"Now there's a story you could tell Gavin to lift his spirits. We were at your Aunt Claire's house in her bedroom, sitting on the floor next to a laundry basket of clean clothes. She reached in and grabbed the first pair of underwear she could find and it was one of Gavin's Spiderman Underoos," I chuckle.

"Shut up, it was not!" Charlotte exclaims, pulling away to look at me.

I nod my head. "Yep, totally was. Your Aunt ripped off the paper backing of the pad and slapped it on the crotch of Spiderman tighty-whities. We decided Kotex was Spiderman's new weapon of choice. Instead of a web shooting out of his wrist, maxi pads would fly out, rendering all of his enemies helpless."

Charlotte and I sat at the kitchen table, reminiscing about the funniest things that have happened over the years and an idea started forming in my head. The one good thing about our group of friends is that we're never short on laughter. Someone is always doing something stupid or inappropriate and no matter what's happening in our lives at that point in time, laughter has always been the cure for everything.

I don't know if I can repair the damage that's been done to my friendship with Claire, but I'm not going down without a fight. We have too many years and too many memories to just give up. Claire has always believed in me and I need to show her that she still can.

Chapter 13

Atom Machine, For the Win!

Nineteen years ago...

"WHERE IN THE hell is Jenny?" I asked Claire, glancing around the casino floor.

She shrugged and put another twenty into the machine in front of her. "I don't know and I don't care. I have found my *Sex in the City* machine and all is right with the world."

When I found out Jim had a meeting for work right next to the casino in Cleveland, Claire decided we should tag along and have a "girls" weekend. We needed it. Claire was running ragged with seven-year-old Gavin and three-year-old Sophie and I was losing my mind with Charlotte, who's also three, Ava who just turned one, and my newborn, Molly, who is six weeks old today. Jenny, being a new mom of only four weeks with her daughter, Veronica, jumped at the chance to get out of the house for a night.

We had entirely too many fucking kids and we needed a break.

We'd only been here for a few hours and we'd already lost Jenny. She had been way too excited about the prospect of free booze while she played. After six rum and cokes during one hand of Black Jack, Claire and I had walked away and pretended like we didn't know her. Luckily, Jim's meeting wasn't until tomorrow morning, so we put him on babysitting duty to make sure she didn't get kicked out of the casino. Bringing a first-time mom who hasn't had a drink in over nine months to a place where you could drink for free as long as you were gambling probably wasn't our brightest idea.

After a few vanilla vodka and diet cokes, I started to feel warm and fuzzy. When I felt warm and fuzzy, I spoke about things that I normally wouldn't when I was sober. Like about how being a mom of three little girls scared the ever living shit out of me.

"So, I'm thinking I'm not cut out to be a mom of three girls. Do you think Jim would be mad if I packed up my things and moved to Lithuania?"

Claire paused with her hand above the "repeat bet" button and turned to look at me. "What in the hell are you talking about?"

I shrugged, smacking my hand down on the closest button on my machine just to give myself something to do. "I mean, this shit is hard. What in the hell ever possessed me to have three kids?"

Not only did I have three kids all under the age of three, I also ran my own business that had turned into several chains across the U.S. and had a husband I liked to pay attention to every once in a while. I was drowning in invoices and baby formula and interviewing preschools and managers for the chains, not to mention the fact that I hadn't gotten more than two consecutive hours of sleep in at least two years.

"Of course it's hard. Being in a mom is the hardest job in the entire fucking world. I'm not going to tell you that 'it's all worth it in the end' or some stupid shit like that because who knows if it will be worth it? Who knows if when our kids finally grow up we'll have done a good job or if they'll need therapy for the rest of their lives? All you can do is the best that you can and believe me, you are doing great. Your kids are all still alive, that's all that matters. If I'm having a shitty day, the kids are crying, the phone is ringing off the hook and Carter and I are arguing about something, all I do is look at my kids and say 'Well, at least they're still alive'," Claire explained.

"I feel like I'm losing my mind. Why didn't you tell me being a mom would make me go insane?"

Claire laughed and shook her head at me. "Sorry, those are trade secrets in the mom world. And if I remember correctly, you were there for the first four years when I was a single mom to a boy who liked to talk about his penis in public. He's seven now and still likes to talk about his penis to strangers, but at least now I have Carter to help out, just like you have Jim. You're doing a great job, Liz. Your girls adore you and someday, they'll be grown and have kids of their own and you can point and laugh at *them* when they come crying to you. Full circle, baby. Full circle."

"DAAAAAAAAADDDY! I need more money!"

Claire and I turned in our seats when we heard Jenny whine behind us. She stood in front of Jim with her hand out while he shook his head at her.

"Uh, hey guys. Why is Jenny calling you daddy?" Claire asked Jim.

Jenny looked up and her sad face immediately went away when she saw us.

"You guys!! I am having the BEST time! But Daddy here took my money and he won't let me have any more," she said with a pout as she pointed at Jim.

My husband stared at her with a blank expression on his face, which usually meant he was trying his hardest to keep his mouth shut before he said something he'd regret.

"Why won't 'DAAAAAADDDDYY' let you have any money?" Claire asked, doing a perfect imitation of Jenny's whiny voice.

"If one more person calls me Daddy, you're all going to die," Jim stated in a monotone voice.

"Daddy isn't being fair!" Jenny complained with a stomp of her foot.

Jim growled and I put a hand on his arm to keep him from choking Jenny.

"Hey, Jenny. How about you tell them why I'm not letting you have your money," Jim suggested.

We looked at Jenny and she rolled her eyes. "I was winning! I put my gambling card in the machine and it gave me two hundred and fifty dollars!"

"What machine is this?" Claire asked, looking around for the machine that was obviously a winner.

"Oh, please tell them what machine," Jim begged, his face suddenly taking on a look of pure delight.

Jenny pointed to the other side of the room. "See? That one over there. The Atom game."

Claire and I squinted, trying to find this Atom game she spoke of, but we couldn't see anything through the mess of people, blinking lights and gaming tables.

"What Jenny is pointing out to you would be the ATM machine," Jim informed us.

"You win every single time!" Jenny announced happily.

"And this is why she is no longer allowed to have her 'gambling card' or her money," Jim added, using his hands to finger-quote gambling card. Which we suddenly realized was her bank card.

"Come on, Daddy! I want to win more money!"

Jenny shouted, grabbing Jim's arm and dragging him away.

He gave us a pleading look, but Claire and I waved happily at him as they disappeared in the crowd.

"Well, the good news is, Jenny is giving him tons of babysitting practice for your kids," Claire stated as I sat back down next to her at my machine. "Would now be a bad time to tell you that I made you and Jim the guardians of Gavin and Sophie if something were to happen to us?"

My hand paused mid-air as I got ready to hit a button on the machine. I stared at her with wide eyes and an open mouth for so long that she finally had to snap her fingers in front of my face to pull me out of my daze.

"Don't worry, it's not like something is going to happen to us," Claire explained. "Carter and I just figured we should update our wills and it's not like I want my dad to get the kids. Could you imagine? They'd spend their childhood watching the Gameshow Network, taking naps and brushing up on their skills of stringing swear words together. Actually, that might not be a bad thing."

"Why in the hell would you ever think it was a good idea to make *me* the guardian of your kids? Did you not just hear me complaining about how I suck as a mother and I don't know what I'm doing?" I reminded her.

Claire turned her chair to face mine. "Listen, going into that lawyers office and having to talk about your children being raised by someone who isn't you is the most depressing thing in the world. I couldn't even get through two minutes of that meeting without crying. My kids drive me insane, but they're still my kids. My *babies*. The thought of not being here to watch them grow and to teach them about life… it really sucks. But as soon as the lawyer asked me for a name, I knew there was no one else in the world I would want to raise my kids if I couldn't do it."

I refused to fucking cry in the middle of a casino, but it was no use. My eyes filled with tears and I was honored that Claire trusted me enough to make me the guardians of her kids, but I still didn't get it.

"But why me? I mean, you have Carter's parents and your dad and, even though Jenny and Drew are fucking crazy, they're fun and young at heart and great parents so far. Why in the hell would you ever pick me?"

Claire cocked her head at me and leaned closer. "No one could ever replace me as my kid's mom. But when you're looking at the people in your life who might just have to take on that role someday, you try to find someone who will give your children a taste of their mother when she's gone, someone who reminds them of you. I can't imagine someone else raising my children. No one seems like the right choice because they're not *me*, so I chose someone who is as close to 'me' as I could get. You're my person, Liz. You're my other half. If I'm not here, there is no one else in the world who could remind my kids of me and give them the same kind of love I did."

"DAAAAAAAAADDDDY! GIVE ME MY GAMBLING CARD! The Atom Machine is hot! Someone just won on it!" we heard Jenny shout over the noise of ringing machines and people cheering.

"And on that note, I think it's time for another drink," Claire announced.

Chapter 14

Aggressive Vagina

IT'S NOT OFTEN that I find myself apologizing to someone, mostly because I make sure I'm never wrong. Just ask my husband. It's tough for someone like me to realize she was an asshole and made a huge mistake. It's even tougher to admit something like that out loud, in front of actual people. Armed with a bag full of tricks, I make my way inside the Cleveland Clinic and head to the Oncology Department on the third floor, prepared to do whatever I can to fix things with Claire. I've spent these last few weeks thinking about our history together and through the good and bad, funny and insane, one thing always remained constant—the fact that Claire and I were meant to be in each other's lives. We were better when we were together. I forced her to be more outgoing and helped her realize her dreams, and she taught me how to not be such a hard ass all the time and take a chance on things like falling in love and being a mother.

After asking a nurse for directions, I finally find the chemo treatment room. Taking a deep breath and making sure the baseball cap is pulled down far enough on my head, I walk inside. I see Carter on the other side of the room, sitting in a chair next to Claire reading a magazine. Claire is curled up under a blanket in a recliner, hooked up to an IV that I'm assuming is the chemo. She's busy doing something on her phone, so I have a second to stare at her without her noticing me. I'm ashamed at myself for not wanting to look at her before because I felt bad or because I was scared. Seeing her now, with a scarf tied around her head and a determined look on her face regardless of what's happening to her, I am so proud to call her my friend. Where before I only noticed her sickness, the pallor of her skin and the loss of her hair, now I see strength. I see what I should have seen all those weeks ago. A woman who takes whatever is thrown at her and pushes through, determined to survive no matter what. A woman who is the strongest person I have ever known. She survived getting pregnant in college and raising a child on her own for four years, she managed to build a thriving business and make her dreams come true, she took care of her family and she always, *always* took care of me. She pushed me to give Jim a chance when I knew nothing about love and relationships, she convinced me I was a good mother and she trusted me to be a good friend no matter what life threw at us.

I walk across the room with my head held high even though I feel like the lowest person in the world. Claire looks up at me in surprise when I drop my bag next to her chair and doesn't say a word as I dig through it for the first item I need. I pull out the piece of paper I printed from the computer this morning, grab a roll of scotch tape and walk over to her IV.

"What are you doing?" Claire finally speaks.

I ignore her for the time being as I tape my sign to the clear bag of fluid hanging from the steel pole next to her chair. When it's finished, I take a step back and study my work.

Carter gets up from his chair and walks over to stand next to me, reading the sign out loud. "This is probably vodka."

He nods his head and pats me on the back. "Fitting. Very fitting."

I walk back to my bag and pull out another sign, taping it to the footrest on her recliner so that it hangs down by Claire's feet. Once again, Carter walks over to me and reads the sign. "Beware: I have an aggressive vagina."

Carter laughs and Claire shoots him a dirty look.

"What?" he asks her. "Your vagina is kind of aggressive."

Next, I pull out a couple of t-shirts, handing one to

Claire. She holds it up in front of her, reading the text printed on the front of it in pink. "Itty Bitty Titty Committee—President".

I hold up my own shirt and she reads it. "Itty Bitty Titty Committee—Secretary."

The third shirt comes out and I turn it around for Claire to read as well. "Itty Bitty Titty Committee—Director of Foreign Affairs."

She looks at me questioningly and I finally speak. "Jenny is the only one of us with a big rack. Obviously she's in charge of Foreign Affairs."

Claire is trying really hard not to smile through her pursed lips and I feel a little better about my plan.

Carter walks over to her side, leans down and kisses the top of her head. "I'm going to head over to the lounge and see if I can find some coffee. Do you need anything?"

Claire shakes her head and Carter gives me a one-armed side hug before he leaves the room, letting me know that he's happy I came.

When we're finally alone, aside from the two other people currently hooked up to their own chemo treatments that are napping on the other side of the room, I stick my hands in my pockets and step closer to Claire's side.

"I'm just going to cut right to the chase and apologize for being an asshole," I tell her. Claire crosses her arms across her chest, not saying a word. "I know nothing that is happening right now is about me, I *know* that, but you're my person, Claire. What happens to you, happens to me. I'm a fixer, I like to make things better, take charge and get shit done. I have never felt so helpless in my life. It killed me that I couldn't do anything to make you better."

Claire opens her mouth to argue with me, but I hold up my hand to stop her. "I know it wasn't up to me. I know it was out of my hands and I should have realized that all you needed was a friend. You needed me and I wasn't there for you. I was too scared, too ashamed, too worried about my own problems to think about what you might need."

I squat down next to her chair and grab her hand, pulling it away from her chest and squeezing it between my two hands. "It's going to be okay, Claire. You're going to be okay. You are a fucking fighter and you're going to beat this."

Her chin quivers and she swipes at a tear that is falling down her cheek and I continue.

"Fuck cancer. Fuck not having your tits anymore because you're going to get bigger and better tits in a few weeks and those fuckers won't try to kill you. You're going to be fine because you *have* to be fine. I refuse to let you NOT be fine because I need you here with me. You are going to beat this thing because you are strong and amazing and you aren't going to let some stupid shit like cancer stop you from growing old with me so we can corrupt our grandchildren. Shit, we have a wedding to finish planning and I have a hotter dress than you to wear to it. You have to be fine because we need to walk down the aisle together so everyone can judge us and realize that I look amazing in my mother of the bride dress."

Claire laughs through her tears and shakes her head at me. "Fuck your face. I'm going to have new tits for this wedding. Obviously I'll be the hotter one."

We stare at each other in silence for a few minutes before she speaks again. "I'm still pissed at you, but I'm glad you're here."

"I'm pissed at me, too. I give you permission to call me an asshole for the rest of our lives," I tell her.

"I was already planning on calling you an asshole forever, this just makes it more fun," Claire says with a shrug. "What else do you have in that bag?"

She leans over the side of her chair and stairs down at my duffle bag.

"There may or may not be some pot Rice Krispies Treats in there."

Claire stares at me wide-eyed, quickly glancing around the room before lowering her voice. "What the fuck are you waiting for? Give me one of those damn things."

Reaching into my bag, I pull out the Tupperware container and hand it to her. She tears open the lid, grabs one of the huge marshmallow squares and shoves the entire thing it into her mouth.

"Um, I don't think you're supposed to eat the whole

thing at once. Didn't you learn your lesson a few years ago with Drew's pot cookies?"

Claire narrows her eyes at me, her cheeks stuffed full of Rice Krispies Treat as she chews slowly. When she finally swallows the thing, she lets out a sigh and smiles at me. "If these things prevent the constant diarrhea and projectile vomiting I'm plagued with after treatment, I will eat the entire fucking container of them. Tunnel vision and licking walls be damned."

"Diarrhea, seriously?" I ask as she grabs another treat and starts chowing down on it.

"Dude, you have no idea. I swear to God I shit out my intestines last time," she informs me. "So, what's been going on since we last talked? I think Carter is losing his shit, but he swears he's okay."

I reach into the container on Claire's lap and take a treat. Friends who get high together, stay together, or some shit like that.

"Your husband absolutely lost his shit all over your kitchen a few weeks back. You'll be happy to know that your non-perishables are no longer in alphabetical order," I tell her. "He's okay though. I think he just needed to get it out of his system. You know, screaming, yelling, cursing God. The boys stopped by and took his mind off of things."

Claire stops chewing. "Is that why my cat now has the word "Fuck Canker" shaved into her side?"

I nod sadly. "Unfortunately, yes. Drew claims she

wouldn't sit still for him long enough to get it right, but I'm pretty sure he thinks that's how you spell cancer. Also, he shaved his legs and my husband shaved his balls. I know you said no one was allowed to shave their heads, so they decided to take a different approach."

Claire shakes her head in irritation. "I'm still holding firm on the spaghetti dinner and candlelight vigil. If any one of you tries that shit, I will stab you in the neck."

"Noted," I tell her with a nod of my head. "Move over."

I stand up as she slides to the other side of her chair, crawling into the recliner next to her.

"Your ass is too big for this chair," she informs me.

"Fuck off, I have a great ass and it's the perfect size," I reply as I get comfortable. "You keep inhaling those Rice Krispies Treats and we're going to have to grease the door to get your giant ass out of here."

Reaching up, I take the baseball cap off of my head, holding onto the scarf I tied underneath to keep it in place.

"So, there's one more thing I have for you and it's really going to piss you off."

Claire looks up from the bowl of treats and stares at my head. Her smile falls and she starts shaking her head frantically back and forth.

"No, you didn't. Fuck your face, NO, YOU DIDN'T!" she yells.

The patients who were previously sleeping wake up

immediately and look in our direction. Reaching up, I squeeze my eyes closed and pull the scarf off of my head, waiting for her to call me an asshole again. When entirely too much time passes without her saying a word, I slowly open my eyes to find Claire outright sobbing. She lifts her hand and runs her palm over my now-bald head.

"I know you hated the tattoo and you're really hating this right now, but it's something I had to do. I realize I can't fix you, but at least I can support you. If you are going to walk around without any hair, then so am I."

Claire continues to rub her palm over my head while she wipes the tears off of her cheeks. "I didn't hate the tattoo, but this is insane."

All I can do is shrug. "Yep, it's totally insane. You need to know that regardless of my actions the last few weeks, there is nothing I wouldn't do for you."

Claire drops her hand into her lap but continues to stare at my shaved head. "I hate to tell you this, but you look like a total asshole, baldy."

I laugh, reaching for the scarf to put it back on my head. Claire puts her hand on top of mine and shakes her head. "Oh, no. Scarf stays off. Also, when I'm done here, we're going to parade you through the grocery store so people will roll their eyes and make snap judgments about your fashion style. I'm going to tell people you're in a gang and make you bark at them."

Claire rests her head on my shoulder and I set my

chin on top of her head. We both stare at the IV, the bag of chemo almost empty. We watch the liquid slowly flow through the tube connected to her PICC line. With each drop that falls, I say a prayer that everything I said to Claire today will come true—that she'll be okay and she'll never leave me.

"I'm sorry," I whisper.

Claire tucks herself in closer to me, grabbing onto my hand and squeezing it. "I know you are."

Carter walks back in the room and does a double-take when he sees my bald head. "Dammit, I knew you'd outdo me. Shaving my balls and pussy isn't as cool anymore."

We ignore the strange stares from the other patients as Carter makes himself comfortable in his chair next to Claire and me.

"You're going to be okay," I remind her.

Claire nods her head. "Yep, I'm totally going to be fine."

For the next half our while she finishes her treatment, our high kicks in and everything suddenly seems so funny that we can't stop giggling. Claire makes me practice my barking for when she takes me to the grocery store and I make her meow like a cat in honor of her poor, shaved pussy at home. I'm pretty sure it's the one and only time someone almost got kicked out of their own chemo treatment.

Things are finally back to normal and aside from the

pot flowing through me, there's also hope. Pot and hope… it doesn't get much better than that.

Chapter 15

Porn Star Tits

Five months later...

"DREW, WHAT THE hell is in that bag?" I ask as he walks into Claire's hospital room, hefting the largest duffle bag I have ever seen on top of the table next to her bed.

"This, my friends, is to prove my theory that size DOES matter," he tells us as he unzips the bag and digs around inside. "I like to call it my Bag O' Boobs."

"Wait, since when did anyone EVER say that size doesn't matter?" Claire asks as we all stare at Drew.

"Since we started talking about your new rack," Drew informs us, pulling out two lemons and holding them up in front of his chest.

Claire finally finished with all of her chemo

treatments two weeks ago and is now undergoing reconstruction surgery. During her mastectomy, the doctor inserted a tissue expander under her skin, but he wanted to wait until her chemo was finished before completing the reconstruction and giving her new boobs. He said that chemo and radiation could sometimes affect implants, so it was easier to just expand the skin on her chest during treatment and then go back and put the implants in when she's done.

"What you have here is your basic A cup. It's budding and beautiful, a perfect small handful and it can get the job done. Since you'd never let me touch your old ones, I'm going by sight alone and I've determined that you were a generous A cup, correct?" Drew asks Claire.

"Oh, good Lord," she mutters.

"Now, why go with what you had before when you can get something new and improved? This is your time, Claire. Your time to make all of my boob dreams come true."

Carter reaches into the bag and pulls out a honeydew melon. Drew immediately snatches it out of his hand and puts it off to the side of the table.

"Now, now, let's not get ahead of ourselves," he scolds.

Drew goes back to the bag and pulls out two oranges. "This here is the next step up. A lovely B cup that is not only ample but alluring."

My husband eyes the oranges and then looks at my

chest, nodding his head. "True story."

I roll my eyes as Drew continues, setting the oranges down and pulling out two grapefruits.

"Next we have the C cup. Full and fabulous. A little more than a handful, but looks great in a bikini."

"I'm suddenly hungry for fruit salad, anyone else?" Jim asks.

Drew ignores him, pulling two cantaloupes out of the bag next.

Jenny walks over and grabs one of them, holding it up to her own boob. "This is me! I have candy loop boobs!"

Drew kisses her cheek, taking the melon back. "Yes, you have lovely candy loops, sweetie pie."

He turns back to face Claire. "D cup. Voluptuous and va-va-va-voom! More than a handful, more than a mouthful and has a delicious, juicy center."

"Eeeeew," I complain.

Jim picks up the honeydew on the table while Drew reaches into the bag and pulls out its match.

"Behold, the double D," Drew says in awe. "Bountiful and bodacious, porn star tits and the star of many a man's fantasy."

Carter and Jim rub their hands over the honeydew with a glazed look in their eyes. I smack the back of both of their heads since Claire is hooked up to an IV in bed and can't reach Carter.

"I love you, your boobs are perfect," Jim tells me sweetly.

"Fuck off," I growl at him.

When the doctor walks in a few minutes later, the boys are in the middle of a heated fruit argument and I'm trying to wrestle the honeydew out of Drew's hands and back in the bag.

"So, Claire. Have you decided on the size? The tissue expander has given us enough skin to work with a full C cup, but it's completely up to you," he explains.

"She'll be going with the honeydew today, doctor," Drew informs him.

This time Carter was the one doing the hitting and Drew let out a yelp when Carter's fist connected with his arm.

"What do you think?" Claire asks Carter.

He shrugs his shoulders. "Babe, I love you exactly the way you are. It is completely up to you."

She narrows her eyes at him and I shake my head. "Stop lying to your wife. Pick a boob size and man up."

Very slowly, Carter leans over to the table and picks up a grapefruit, looking at Claire sheepishly. "Um, this is kind of nice."

I give him a pat on the back. "Well done, sir."

Claire lets out a sigh and smiles. "I guess we'll be going with the grapefruit today, doctor."

The doctor spends a few minutes chatting with Claire about the procedure and making notes on her chart before he leaves the room. Jenny, Drew, Jim and Carter go in search of coffee while Claire moves over in bed, patting the empty spot next to her. I hop up beside her, grabbing the extra grapefruit and holding it up in front of her chest.

"I'm going to have to fire you from your position as president of the Itty Bitty Titty Club. This is a sad, sad day in Titty Club history," I tell her sadly.

"I'd like to say I'm sorry for stepping down from this illustrious position, but I'm not. I'm going to have FANTASTIC tits!" Claire announces.

"I hate you. You're going to look so much better in your mother of the groom dress next month."

"Fuck the dress, I'm going to walk around naked from now on. Show my tits to people when I'm walking down the street. I might even ask random strangers to touch them," she tells me.

"You could even make up a new cupcake for the store. Tantalizing Titty Cakes."

She nods her head. "Creamy C Cup-Cakes. With a milky filling."

I dry heave and shake my head. "Too far. Jesus God, too far."

"Will you still love me even when I have a better rack than you?" she asks.

I wrap my arm around her shoulder and nod. "I love you when you're an asshole, I love you when I'm an asshole, I love you when you have no hair and I love you when you call me on my shit. Of course I'll still love you when you have better tits than me. I'll secretly hate you on the inside, but it will be fine."

We settle back into the pillows and stare up at the ceiling where I taped random notes while she was in the bathroom earlier changing into her hospital gown. It reminds me of that time in college when we got drunk on Boone's Farm and curled up on our bunk bed, staring at my stickers taped to the bottom of the bunk.

"I think the one that says 'Hot Tits or Bust' is my favorite," Claire states.

"I don't know, I'm particularly fond of the My Little Pony with the huge rack," I tell her. "Pinky Pie Porn Star is all the rage."

Claire laughs. "I told you My Little Pony would make a comeback."

"And I told you that you would be okay, didn't I?" I remind her.

"You did. And you were right," she tells me with a nod.

"I'm always right. Except with the whole shaving my head thing. That was probably a bad move."

I run my hands over my short, spiky blonde hair that Claire would not let me continue shaving after the first time. She demanded that I let it grow back out immediately. I now resemble that chick from the movie *The Legend of Billie Jean* and I'm pretty sure Claire just wanted me to start growing it out so she could quote that damn movie every time she saw me.

She puts her fist in the air and shouts, "FAIR IS FAIR!"

I roll my eyes. "Stop being an asshole."

"Shut up, YOU'RE an asshole," she counters.

"But I'm your little asshole and I promise, I will never get spooked again," I tell her solemnly.

"Now you're REALLY an asshole for quoting *Cocktail.* Just sit there and be quiet and let's dream about my new, pretty boobs," she tells me as she closes her eyes.

"I get to touch them first," I remind her.

She scoffs. "Obviously."

Epilogue

NOT EVERYONE HANDLES bad news the same way. Some people scream and cry and rage about the unfairness of it all, others turn all emo and clam up and refuse to accept reality and some continue to have hope and fill their days with rainbows and unicorns and never let the man bring them down.

Then you have me. I thought I could fix everything until life gave us something unexpected that I could do nothing about. My friendship with Claire was tested and I'm happy to say we came out stronger on the other side. Claire now has a better rack than me and her hair is finally starting to grow back.

The doctors are confident that they removed all of the cancer from her body during the mastectomy and the chemo was done as a preventative measure for insurance. There's always a chance that some of the cancer cells traveled elsewhere in her body and we won't really know anything definitive for a while, but Claire is happy, she feels great and that's good enough for all of us. We have a wedding next month to finish planning and we're not going to let a little bit of cancer get in our way. Claire's illness forced us all to realize just how fragile life really is and that we can't take one minute for granted. She went with me last week to get my first mammogram and I've already scheduled my next follow-up appointment. Jenny and Drew continue to play "mammogram" at home in between her own appointments. Even though just the thought of it is disgusting, at least she's being proactive.

Tantalizing Titty Cakes have been a huge hit at Seduction and Snacks. We give them away for free on days when Claire has a doctor's appointment and she also has a stash of "special" Titty Cakes hidden under the counter for cancer patients and cancer survivors. They get an entire dozen for free, along with a warning to only eat a little bit at a time unless they want to start crawling on countertops, thinking the wallpaper tastes like

Snozzberries and barking like a dog in the middle of chemo treatments.

Through it all, we're staying positive and we are absolutely keeping our sense of humor.

I think people sometimes forget just how powerful laughter is. I know I did for a little while. It took a trip down memory lane to remind me that the best thing about our group of friends is our ability to make each other laugh, even in awful situations. Sometimes you just need to pretend like your IV is filled with vodka, get a horrible rack of ribs tattoo on your body and almost get kicked out of a hospital for filling out their information form with porn titles. Life is filled with enough bullshit and drama, why make it worse? Tell me something. What makes you feel better, crying and complaining or laughing and making fun of a situation? It's an easy answer and one we all need to remember from time to time. Cancer definitely isn't a laughing matter, but what are a few giggles and a couple of inappropriate comments going to hurt? Sure, you might get some funny looks when you're at a funeral or in an ICU ward at a hospital, but that's just because those people haven't learned what *you* have—laughter makes everything better. It might not cure cancer, but it sure makes it a hell of a lot more bearable.

Fuck Cancer. Save second base. Fight like a girl. Do it all and do it with a few laughs because you are amazing, you are strong and you are a fighter, just like my best friend.

The End

Turn the page for more information about breast cancer awareness.

Statistics

- There are nearly three million breast cancer survivors in the U.S.

- One in eight women in the U.S. will be diagnosed with breast cancer in her lifetime.

- Early detection and effective treatment have resulted in a 34 percent decline in breast cancer in the U.S. since 1990.

- Worldwide, breast cancer is the most frequently diagnosed cancer and the leading cause of cancer death in women.

- Every 19 seconds, somewhere in the world, a case of breast cancer is diagnosed in a woman.

- Every minute, somewhere in the world, someone dies from breast cancer.

- Breast cancer knows no boundaries—be it age, gender, socio-economic status or geographic location.

Information courtesy of Susan G. Komen
http://ww5.komen.org/

Acknowledgements

My deepest gratitude goes to Claire Contreras. You are the strongest, most beautiful person inside and out and I love you! Thank you so much for sharing your journey with me and making sure I got all the facts straight.

To Donna and Nikki—thank you for lighting a fire under my ass and making sure I did this. I promise I won't call you whores anymore. Well, I'll still call Donna a whore, sorry.

For Stephanie Johnson for always being on board whenever I say, "So, you want to read something?" Thank you for supporting me and for being a wonderful friend, my beautiful Cookie Whore.

To Nikole Lasky, my sister from another mister. Thank you for your help in remembering all the stupid shit we did when Nana was sick. It's tough getting old. Thank you for being my partner in crime and helping me almost get kicked out of entirely too many hospitals for our loud, inappropriate behavior. The next time I blow the sugar from a packet, I'll make sure to remove my hospital mask so I don't look like an asshole and embarrass you.

For Mom, Grandma, Jill, Ellen and Aunt Kathy. Fighters and survivors and the strongest women I was ever blessed to be related to.

Last, but not least, for my best friend, MY person— Buffy. This story would not have been possible without you because I never would have known what it was like to have a true friend, my other half, someone who *gets* me so completely, if I'd never met you. There would be no Claire and Liz without you because we ARE Claire and Liz. I am here, always and forever, all you have to do is call. Sometimes I'll be a bitch, and sometimes you'll be an asshole, but we will always cut someone's mother for each other and that's how it should be. I am lucky to have been given two soul mates in my life, and even luckier that you are one of them. I love you, asshole.

Made in the USA
Middletown, DE
17 October 2014